John Harrold.

CONTENTS

STORIES BY IAN ROBINSON
ILLUSTRATED BY JOHN HARROLD
STORY COLOURING BY GINA HART

This book belongs to:

....

....

John Harrold.

THE EXPRESS ANNUAL

RUPERT

John Harrold.

Pedigree®
BOOKS

No 63

Published by Pedigree Books Limited
The Old Rectory, Matford Lane, Exeter, EX2 4PS.

£6.99
RU63

RUPERT and

One morning, Mrs. Bear says, "We Have asked your cousin Joan to tea . . ."

Rupert sets out to get some more Provisions from the village store.

One morning, Rupert is busy playing in his room when Mrs. Bear asks if he would like to help her with some baking . . . "Aunt Emma and Cousin Joan are coming to visit us this afternoon, so I thought we'd make a batch of butterfly cakes. I remember how much Joan enjoyed them last time she came!" Rupert always likes helping in the kitchen and happily agrees to join his mother. "Butterfly cakes are one of my favourites too!" he smiles.

Mrs. Bear goes to the kitchen and writes out a shopping list of all the things they will need. She gives Rupert a basket and asks him to go into Nutwood to fetch them from Mr. Chimp's store. "Eggs, flour and butter are the most important ingredients when you're baking," she says. "We could do with some more icing sugar too, if he's got any . . . I'll switch the oven on to heat and get everything ready while you're gone."

the Missing Cakes

*"My Mum's having a baking day -
She needs all these things, straightaway . . ."*

*"Eggs, butter and some flour as well
But what sort is it? I can't tell!"*

Rupert sets off along the path to Nutwood. "I'd better hurry!" he thinks. "I don't want to keep Mum waiting . . ." When he arrives at the village store, Mr. Chimp reads through his shopping list and smiles. "I see Mrs. Bear's having a baking day!" "That's right!" says Rupert. "Aunt Emma and Cousin Joan are coming to stay. We're going to make some butterfly cakes!" "Very nice too!" nods the grocer. "Just the thing for afternoon tea . . ."

Mr. Chimp starts to load everything into Rupert's basket, carefully counting out a dozen fresh eggs from a big bowl on the counter . . . When they get to flour, he stops and blinks in surprise. "No labels!" he declares. "That's very odd. There must have been a mix-up at the mill. I can't tell if it's plain flour, self-raising flour or strong flour, for baking bread. The bags are different colours, but there isn't anything to tell us which is which . . ."

RUPERT MAKES SOME CAKES

Which bag of flour should Rupert take?
"I think it's blue to make a cake . . ."

"Well done!" says Mrs. Bear. "Now we
Can make a start immediately!"

His mother teaches Rupert how
To make a cake. "Keep stirring now!"

"These small cakes don't take long to cook.
They're done already, Rupert, look!"

Which bag of flour should Rupert choose? "The blue one!" he decides. "I'm sure that's the colour we normally have." "Good!" says Mr. Chimp. "If blue is self-raising, then red must be plain. One is for baking cakes, while the other is for making pastry. You mustn't use the wrong one, or your cakes won't rise. They'll all be flat as pancakes!" As soon as he has filled his basket, Rupert sets off home as quickly as he can. "Well done!" says Mrs. Bear. "Now we can make a start . . ."

In the Bears' kitchen, Rupert's mother has already looked out a large mixing bowl. Measuring all the ingredients carefully, she gives Rupert a spoon and asks him to stir them together. "Perfect!" she smiles. "Now we need to fill a baking tray and pop it in the oven . . ." Although the cakes won't take long to cook, Rupert can hardly wait. "I hope I chose the right flour!" he thinks. "Otherwise, they'll never rise . . ." "Wonderful!" says Mrs. Bear at last. "They've turned out very well."

RUPERT MEETS HIS COUSIN JOAN

The cakes cool down and Rupert tries
To turn them into butterflies . . .

"We'll try them later!" says his Mum,
"When Joan and Emma's train has come . . ."

At Nutwood station, Rupert hears
A whistle, "It's the train!" he cheers.

Aunt Emma and Joan wave, then call,
"How wonderful to see you all!"

When the cakes have cooled, Mrs. Bear shows Rupert how to turn them into butterflies . . . First they make a bowl of sweet, creamy filling, then slice the top off each little cake. "Cut each top in half, then set them like wings," says Rupert's mother. "That's the way! I'm sure that Joan will love them!" Rupert's cousin is not the only one who likes butterfly cakes . . . "Those look delicious!" says Mr. Bear. "Come on!" calls his wife. "Time we were off! You can try a cake later."

As Rupert and his parents arrive at Nutwood station they can hear the shrill whistle of an approaching train. "It's here already!" calls Rupert excitedly. "I can't wait to see Joan . . ." "Hello!" calls Aunt Emma. "How nice to be back in Nutwood! It's such a lovely village. Goodness, Rupert, I think you've grown!" Rupert's little cousin is delighted to be in Nutwood too. "What fun!" says Joan. "We're going to be staying for a whole weekend. It's just like going on holiday!"

RUPERT IS AMAZED

"I do like Nutwood! What a sight!"
Says Emma, beaming with delight . . .

Then Joan spots something flying by,
"It looks just like a butterfly!"

Rupert's amazed. "A flying cake!
Just like the ones I helped to make . . ."

He hurries indoors eagerly,
"This way, Joan. Quickly! Follow me . . ."

"Isn't Nutwood peaceful!" says Aunt Emma as the Bears walk home from the station. "No busy roads, no big factories, just trees and fields and lovely houses, like yours . . ." Rupert and Joan follow the others, happily making plans for the next few days. "I hope the weather stays fine," begins Rupert, then breaks off as his cousin points to something excitedly. "Look at that huge butterfly!" she cries. "I've never seen anything like it . . ."

As Rupert stares up in astonishment, a second object comes fluttering over the hedge. "Those aren't butterflies!" he tells Joan. "They're cakes! The butterfly cakes we were going to have for tea . . ." "Flying cakes?" blinks Joan. "I've never heard of those before!" "Neither have I!" says Rupert. "Something very strange must have happened. We'd better go and see . . ." Hurrying forward, he dashes through the front door, with his astonished cousin following close behind.

RUPERT CHASES THE FLYING CAKES

*The kitchen window's open wide
And all the cakes have flown outside . . .*

*"No time to explain!" Rupert cries.
"We're off to catch some butterflies!"*

*The cakes all fly off through the air,
Pursued by the astonished pair . . .*

*The chums are both determined they
Won't let their quarry get away!*

Running into the kitchen, Rupert is just in time to see the last of the butterfly cakes disappearing out of the window. "Oh, no!" he cries. "I must have used the wrong sort of flour after all . . ." "It's magic!" gasps Joan. "The cakes are all following each other!" "You're right!" says Rupert. "I wonder where they're going?" He hurries back through the front door and past his startled parents. "No time to explain!" he calls. "Another minute and they'll all be gone!"

Hurrying to the end of the path, Rupert is just in time to see the butterfly cakes flying off over Nutwood common. "Follow me!" he calls to Joan. "We mustn't let them get out of sight!" The pair run as fast as they can, but the cakes are too swift to catch. "They're heading towards the Upper common!" cries Rupert. "Perhaps it's just a breeze that's blowing them along?" "I wonder?" says Joan. "If you ask me, they're following each other. Like birds in Winter, when they fly South . . ."

RUPERT AND JOAN GET LOST

"A stream!" calls Joan. "Is it too wide
Or can we reach the other side?"

The cakes fly on, then Rupert sees
Them swooping down, towards some trees . . .

"Quick, Joan!" calls Rupert. "Follow me!
There's one last cake that I can see . . ."

The pair run fast, but soon find they
Are lost and cannot tell the way!

Following the cakes across the common, Rupert and his cousin come to a narrow stream. "Do you think we can get across?" asks Joan. "Let's see!" laughs Rupert. Leaping to the far bank, he scrambles ashore. "Bravo!" he cheers as Joan jumps over to join him. "Now, where are those flyaway cakes?" Peering into the distance, the pair spot their quarry, fluttering into a wood by the edge of the common. "Good!" calls Rupert. "The trees should slow them down . . ."

Rupert and Joan reach the edge of the forest just as the last of the cakes disappears into a tangle of trees . . . "This way!" calls Rupert. "We'll follow the path!" At first the way through the wood seems clear, but with each twist and turn the pair grow more confused. "Which way now?" asks Joan. "I can't see any cakes!" "Neither can I!" admits Rupert. "There seem to be paths all over the wood. We'd better not go too far or we might not be able to find our way back!"

12

RUPERT FINDS A STRANGE HOUSE

Then Rupert's cousin gives a cry,
"Look! I can see a butterfly . . ."

"Well done, Joan!" Rupert starts to cheer,
Then gasps, "It's real!" as they get near.

The pair spot woodsmoke in the sky -
"A chimney! There's a house nearby . . ."

They reach a clearing - Rupert blinks,
"Just like a loaf of bread!" he thinks.

Just as the chums are about to turn back, Joan spots something fluttering by the edge of a clearing. "Look!" she calls excitedly. "It's one of the cakes. We must have been going the right way, after all . . ." Rupert catches a glimpse of the distant object. "Well done!" he calls. "This time we won't let it get away!" Running through the wood, he suddenly stops with a gasp of surprise. "A real butterfly!" he cries. "It only *looked* like a flying cake."

Disappointed at giving up the chase, Rupert has a last look round for any sign of the flyaway cakes. To his surprise, he spots a wisp of smoke, curling up into the sky. "A chimney!" he murmurs. "I didn't know there were any houses in the middle of the forest." Overcome with curiosity, the cousins push through the trees until they reach a large clearing with a strange cottage in the middle. "How odd!" blinks Rupert. "It looks just like a giant loaf of bread!"

RUPERT KNOCKS AT THE DOOR

"Let's see who lives here. They might know
Where all the woodland pathways go . . ."

The owner says, "Hello! I'm sure
*I've never seen **you** here before . . ."*

"Keep following the path: it takes
*You to a town that's **full** of cakes!"*

The cousins set off nervously,
"Wherever can this strange town be?"

Although the cottage looks like a loaf of bread, everything else about it seems to be quite normal. "The smoke from the chimney means there must be someone inside," says Rupert. "Let's see if they have spotted any flying cakes." He knocks at the door and waits for a reply. For a long time nothing happens, then the door swings open, revealing a kindly-looking old lady. "Hello!" she says, peering out at the cousins. "I don't think I've seen *you* before. I hope you haven't lost your way?"

When the old lady hears Rupert's story she smiles and shakes her head. "Flying cakes?" she laughs. "That's something I've *never* seen! Pancakes, perhaps, but flying cakes, dear me!" Seeing the chums' disappointment, she points out a path to the nearest village. "That's the place to look for cakes!" she nods. "All shapes and sizes there!" Taking her advice, Rupert and Joan set off along the winding track. "I can't see any houses!" whispers Joan. "Perhaps we should turn back?"

14

RUPERT MEETS A MUFFIN-MAN

*The chums meet someone on the way -
A muffin-seller with a tray . . .*

*He greets the pair and Rupert tries
To ask about the butterflies . . .*

*"Our town is full of different cakes -
You'll find that **everybody** bakes . . ."*

*"A town of bakers! Now we'll see
Where all the missing cakes must be . . ."*

Before Rupert and Joan can decide what to do, they hear a distant call, "Muffins, fresh muffins!" "I can hear a bell!" declares Joan. "Look, Rupert. There's someone coming this way . . ." Spotting the cousins, the muffin-man rings his bell and gives a cheery smile. "Hello!" he calls. "Good afternoon! You're on the right path if you want the town . . ." "Thank you," says Rupert. "What we *really* want are butterfly cakes. You haven't seen any, have you?"

"Butterfly cakes?" laughs the man. "Muffins are more my line but you've certainly come to the right place! We're all bakers in Cakeville. There are people who make bread, people who bake buns, biscuit-makers, pastry cooks and pie-men. The whole town's baking from dawn to dusk! You can tell by the windmills how much flour we use." "I wonder if that's where Nutwood's flour comes from too?" murmurs Rupert. "Come on, Joan! Let's go and see."

RUPERT DISCOVERS CAKEVILLE

"They're all cake buildings!" Rupert cries,
Unable to believe his eyes . . .

As they explore, the cousins find
Shops filled with cakes of every kind.

Each window that the pair walk by
Is filled with lovely cakes to try!

A man looks out. "Hello there! I'm
So glad you found us - Just in time!"

When Rupert and Joan reach Cakeville, they can hardly believe their eyes . . . "The buildings look like giant cakes!" gasps Rupert. "They're the same as the old lady's house!" "These are much more fun!" laughs Joan. "They're covered in icing, with cherries on the roof!" Entering the town, the pair find its streets thronged with bakers and delivery boys, carrying trays and baskets, while all the shop windows are piled high with cakes and buns.

The cakes in the shop windows are so delicious that Rupert and Joan can't resist stopping for a closer look. "Chocolate cake!" says Joan. "That's my favourite . . ." "Mine too!" laughs Rupert. "I wonder what it's like?" At that moment, a man dressed in a long white apron appears and urges the pair to come inside. "Glad you've arrived!" he calls. "I was beginning to think you must have lost the way. It gets rather hectic on Baking Days in Cakeville . . ."

RUPERT MEETS MR. BUNN

He leads the pair inside the shop.
"This way now, please. No time to stop!"

"You'll need to both get changed now, please.
We wear aprons and hats, like these . . ."

"Here's Mr. Crust, my Number Two,
He'll show you youngsters what to do . . ."

"Ah! New recruits!" the old man beams.
He thinks they're trainee cooks, it seems . . .

Inside the baker's shop, Rupert and Joan can smell fresh bread, delicious cakes and marzipan sweets. To their surprise, they find themselves being hurried past the counter towards the kitchens. "First things first!" says the man. "You'll both need aprons and hats. We all wear those in the bakery . . . I'm Mr. Bunn, the Head Baker. As soon as you're ready I'll take you to meet the rest of my staff." "Staff?" blinks Rupert. "Yes!" says Mr. Bunn. "They'll all be delighted to see you!"

Mr. Bunn leads Rupert and Joan to the kitchens, where a group of bakers and pastry chefs are working busily. "Mr. Crust will look after you!" he declares. "I can't stay any longer, I'm afraid. Baking Days are always a rush!" "Pleased to meet you!" smiles the second baker. "Glad you could come and help us at such short notice." "Help?" blinks Rupert. "I think there's been some sort of mix-up . . ." "That's right!" nods the man. "We'll start with Mixing, then see how you're getting on."

RUPERT BECOMES A BAKER

*The pair decide to try their best
And mix up bread dough, like the rest . . .*

*A bell rings out, and instantly
The bakers all stop - "Time for tea!"*

*"While all the bakers have their break
We'll tell them we're here by mistake!"*

*"Although we think cake-making's fun
We're not real trainees, Mr. Bunn!"*

The bakers seem so busy that Rupert and Joan decide to help them anyway . . . "It's just like making cakes with Mum!" says Rupert. "Hard work though! This dough takes some stirring!" "I hope mine's right!" says Joan. "How will we know when to stop?" "Let's ask Mr. Crust," says Rupert, but at that very moment a bell rings and *all* the bakers stop work. "Time for a tea-break!" smiles the old man. "How are you two youngsters enjoying yourselves? You've made a good start."

As the men all gather round for tea, Rupert spots Mr. Bunn and decides to tell him about the flying butterfly cakes . . . "Hello!" smiles the baker. "You've made a good start, I hear! Old Crust thinks you'll both make splendid apprentices." "But we're not!" says Rupert. "There's been a bit of a mix-up, I'm afraid. We didn't come to Cakeville to learn about making cakes at all. We've come here to *catch* them . . ." "Catch cakes?" blinks the baker. "Whatever do you mean?"

RUPERT IS GIVEN A PRESENT

The baker listens with surprise
To Rupert's tale of butterflies . . .

"You used this flour - that's what went wrong,
*It's specially milled - and **very** strong!"*

"I'm sorry, Rupert. I'm afraid
You'll never find the cakes you made . . ."

"Don't worry! Here's some more to try -
*I guarantee that **they** won't fly!"*

To Mr. Bunn's amazement, Rupert tells the whole story of how his butterfly cakes flew out of the window and all the way to Cakeville . . . "Goodness!" he smiles. "You must have used Bakers' Flour!" Taking a packet from a nearby shelf, he explains that it is too strong for everyday baking, but sometimes used as a secret ingredient by bakeries. "It's very important not to use too much! I remember once, we had a whole batch of sponge cakes take off, just like flying saucers!"

When Mr. Bunn learns that Rupert and Joan have come all the way from Nutwood, he says he'll arrange for a delivery man to take them home. "I'm afraid there's not much chance of finding your cakes!" he declares. "They're probably *miles* away by now . . ." Thanking the pair for their help, he leads them into the shop and produces a large box. "How about some new cakes to take back to Nutwood? I wouldn't like to think of visitors to Cakeville going home empty-handed!"

RUPERT MAKES A DELIVERY

The baker hails a nearby van,
"I call at Nutwood!" says the man.

The cousins set off- homeward bound,
"Nutwood's the first stop on my round!"

"Look!" Rupert calls excitedly.
"That's Nutwood's church tower we can see!"

At Mr. Chimp's the pair say they
Will carry in the baker's tray . . .

Outside the shop, the streets are still busy with delivery boys and busy bakers. "I say!" calls Mr. Bunn. "Anyone going to Nutwood?" "Just leaving!" says a driver and happily agrees to take Rupert and Joan along too. "We often make deliveries to Nutwood!" the man smiles as they start the homeward journey. "Mr. Chimp is one of my regular customers." "Amazing!" blinks Rupert. "I'd no idea where all our cakes and bread came from. You must deliver to all the nearby villages . . ."

The baker's van speeds away from Cakeville and is soon on the road to Nutwood. "There's the village!" cries Rupert. "It doesn't seem far when you're driving!" laughs the man. "Walking through the forest must have taken you two ages." When they reach Mr. Chimp's shop the driver stops and opens the van doors to take out Nutwood's cakes. "Special delivery!" he laughs as the grocer comes hurrying out. "I've brought some new assistants with me!"

He hears their tale, and then learns why
The cakes that Rupert made could fly . . .

The cousins run back eagerly -
"We'll have the new cakes for our tea!"

"Let's try the cakes now, everyone!"
"Bravo!" calls Mrs. Bear. "Well done!"

"If only they knew!" Rupert thinks.
He smiles at Cousin Joan, and winks . . .

Mr. Chimp is amazed to hear that Rupert and Joan have been to Cakeville. He is even *more* astonished by their tale of flying cakes. "It's all to do with those unmarked bags of flour!" Rupert tells him. "I'd send them back to the mill if I were you . . ." Leaving the bewildered grocer, the two cousins hurry back to Rupert's house with their box of cakes from Mr. Bunn. "I hope we haven't missed tea!" says Joan. "Everyone must be wondering where we are!"

Arranging the new cakes on a plate, Rupert carries them in to his parents, who are still chatting happily with Aunt Emma . . . "Well done!" says Mrs. Bear. "I was just telling everyone how much you enjoyed our baking day." "These cakes are delicious!" declares Rupert's Aunt. "You ought to be a pastry cook!" "Perhaps he will, one day!" laughs Joan. "Mr. Crust could carry on teaching both of us, as his latest pair of apprentices . . ."

THE END

RUPERT and

*One fine spring morning Rupert goes
In search of all the pals he knows.*

One fine spring morning Rupert decides to go for a walk on Nutwood common. "I wonder if I'll meet anyone?" he thinks. "Bill and Algy might be playing football." As he carries on, Rupert notices a little bird. It hovers above him for a moment then swoops down purposefully. To Rupert's surprise, it calls his name. "Thank goodness I've found you! Odmedod the scarecrow asked me to deliver an important message . . ."

the Goose Chase

*A bird flies down. "Rupert! I've come
From Odmedod, your scarecrow chum . . ."*

*"What Odmedod told me to say,
Was, can you please come straightaway?"*

The bird tells Rupert that Odmedod wants to see him. "Something strange has happened at the farm!" it explains. Rupert agrees to come at once. "Odmedod is in the far field," the bird chirps. "He couldn't come and find you himself in case anyone saw!" Rupert follows the bird across the fields towards Farmer Brown's. After a while he spots a familiar figure standing in the distance. "Good!" says the bird. "Nobody else is there."

*The scarecrow stands upon a hill
He doesn't move but keeps quite still . . .*

*"Hello!" says Odmedod. "I knew
You'd come if I sent word to you . . ."*

*"I didn't want to cause alarm
But something's happened at the farm!"*

*"A stranger came and, so I'm told,
He spoke of goose eggs made from gold . . ."*

*"It sounds unlikely but those two
Seem quite convinced it might be true!"*

Rupert hurries across the field to Odmedod. "Hello!" calls the scarecrow. "Sorry to bother you, but I've made a strange discovery I think you should know about . . ." To Rupert's astonishment, Odmedod looks all round then starts to whisper. "A stranger came to the farm a few days ago and was asking lots of questions about the geese!" "Geese?" blinks Rupert. "Yes," says Odmedod. "He thought that one of them was different from all the others. He claimed it could lay golden eggs!"

"A goose that lays golden eggs?" marvels Rupert. "It sounds like a fairy tale." "That's what I thought!" nods Odmedod. "The odd thing is, a new goose has arrived on the farm. Mollie and Mildred saw it crossing the yard." "Mollie?" asks Rupert. The scarecrow points to a pair of horses in the next field. "Their stables are near the farmhouse so they see everything that happens . . ." The horses tell Rupert that the new goose looks just like all the others but seems very shy.

RUPERT GOES TO THE FARM

*"I'll go and see what I can find -
I'm sure that Farmer Brown won't mind . . ."*

*"Another visitor! I'm sure
I've never seen their car before . . ."*

*"Two men came earlier to see
If they could buy goose eggs from me . . ."*

*A sudden honking fills the air -
"That's Gertie! She might peck the pair!"*

Intrigued by Odmedod's story, Rupert decides to go to the farm and see the new goose for himself. "I wonder if it really can lay golden eggs?" he thinks. "Mrs. Brown will know if anyone does. I'll ask her if she's seen anything strange." As Rupert reaches the farm, he spots an odd-looking car parked in the courtyard. "I've never seen that before!" he blinks. "Perhaps it's one of the Professor's new inventions. I wonder if he has heard about the new goose too?"

When Rupert reaches the farmhouse he calls to ask Mrs. Brown what has been happening. "It's all very odd!" she shrugs. "A man came to talk about geese the other day and now he's back, together with his servant. They want to buy a basket of eggs." Rupert is about to ask more when he hears a sudden commotion from the other side of the yard. "The geese!" gasps Mrs. Brown. "They sound angry about something. I hope those men are safe. They'll get pecked if they upset Gertie."

RUPERT SEES HUMPHREY PUMPHREY

"Sir Humphrey Pumphrey!" Rupert blinks.
"He must be after gold!" he thinks . . .

"Don't worry! It's a false alarm.
The noisy geese have done no harm."

"Sir Humphrey's had no luck, I see . . .
I wonder what the truth can be?"

Rupert explores, intrigued to find
A single goose that's stayed behind.

As Rupert and Mrs. Brown cross the farmyard, two men appear, pursued by angry geese! "Sir Humphrey Pumphrey!" gasps Rupert. "He must be the stranger the horses saw. I wonder if he's found any golden eggs?" "Goodness!" exclaims the farmer's wife. "I hope you haven't been injured! I must apologise for Gertie's behaviour." "No need to worry!" says Sir Humphrey. "Scrogg and I have got all the eggs we need. I expect the geese just aren't used to visitors."

Rupert watches thoughtfully as Humphrey Pumphrey goes back to his car. "I'm sure he's after the goose that lays golden eggs!" he thinks. "I expect he wants to put it in his private zoo . . ." Still not sure what to make of Odmedod's story, he decides to take a closer look in the goose-hut. At first Rupert thinks the geese have all gone, but, as he steps inside, he suddenly spots one hiding in the straw. "Don't worry!" he whispers. "I won't give you away . . ."

RUPERT MEETS A SPECIAL GOOSE

The goose looks up. "No need to fear,
But I know why you're hiding here . . ."

"Hello!" says Gertie. "Don't say you
Have come to look for goose eggs too?"

"A golden egg! It's really true!
No wonder Pumphrey's after you . . ."

"He's not the only one, you know!
*Men chase me **everywhere** I go!"*

Although the goose looks just like all the others, Rupert feels certain it is the one Sir Humphrey has been looking for . . . "Odmedod the scarecrow told me all about you," he explains. "I didn't believe him at first, but now I think the stories must be true . . ." As Rupert speaks, Gertie and the other geese come waddling back, still laughing at the way they saw off Scrogg and Sir Humphrey. "Rupert!" she blinks. "What are you doing here? Don't say you've come looking for eggs as well!"

Rupert tells the geese he has come to warn them about Sir Humphrey and his zoo. "Thank you!" sighs the golden goose. "Everywhere I go, people are after me. Always for the same reason . . ." Pointing to a nest in the straw she shows Rupert a gleaming gold egg. "We've done what we can to help," says Gertie. "But I don't think we've seen the last of Sir Humphrey Pumphrey!" "You're right!" nods Rupert. "We'll have to make a plan in case he comes back . . ."

RUPERT IS WORRIED

The farmyard geese tell Rupert how
They'll all be on the look-out now . . .

"Sir Humphrey and his friend just paid
For every egg our geese had laid!"

"There must be something I can do
To save the goose from Pumphrey's zoo . . ."

As Rupert wanders home he hears
A call. The Sage of Um appears!

Rupert promises the geese that he will come back and see them again as soon as he has thought of a plan. "In the meanwhile we'll all keep a look-out!" says Gertie. "If anyone spots Sir Humphrey they'll raise the alarm by honking as loud as they can." Mrs. Brown tells Rupert that the visitors bought a whole basket of eggs and said they might be back later in the week for more. "I can't understand why they want so many!" she exclaims. "One goose egg is just like another!"

As Rupert walks back from the farm, he thinks of how Sir Humphrey Pumphrey will stop at nothing to get what he wants . . . "There must be *something* I can do to help the golden goose!" he sighs. "It isn't safe for it to stay on the farm." Just then, Rupert hears a cheery call and looks up to see the Sage of Um, in his flying Brella. "Hello!" cries the visitor. "I was just on my way home from Nutwood when I suddenly spotted you walking along. Wait there and I'll come down for a chat."

RUPERT'S FRIEND HAS AN IDEA

The Sage of Um says, "Tell me why
You looked perplexed as I flew by . . ."

He hears about the golden goose -
And how Sir Humphrey's on the loose!

"I know! The golden goose can come
And live in peace with me, on Um . . . !"

"We'll go and let your parents know -
I'm sure they won't mind if you go."

The Sage of Um is a wise old man who lives on a faraway island, together with the last herd of unicorns in the world. He has often helped Rupert before and listens carefully to his story about the goose and Sir Humphrey Pumphrey . . . "Such a creature would be a great prize!" he frowns. "You're right to be concerned. Sir Humphrey will keep searching, especially if he thinks the other geese have something to hide. We need to think of somewhere else for the goose to stay!"

Rupert and the Sage think hard for a moment, then both come up with the same answer . . . "Um Island!" laughs Rupert's friend. "The goose will be safe from Sir Humphrey there. Hardly anyone knows where to find Um and it never appears on maps." The Sage suggests that Rupert should tell the goose their plan and accompany it on the journey. "First, we must go and ask your parents," he declares. "I'm sure they won't mind when they hear why you want to go . . ."

RUPERT RETURNS TO THE FARM

"Yes," Mrs. Bear smiles. "I agree!
But only if you stay for tea . . ."

The pair set out, but as they go
The sun sets with an orange glow.

"I'll wait here," says the Sage. "Look out!
There may be people still about . . ."

Rupert creeps forward silently.
"Hello!" he says. "It's only me!"

Mr. and Mrs. Bear are pleased to see the Sage and happily agree to Rupert visiting Um Island. "I hope you'll stay for tea before you go!" says Rupert's mother. "I want to hear all about the unicorns . . ." The sky is darkening by the time Rupert and his friend set out for Farmer Brown's, but the Sage seems unconcerned. "It's probably as well for the goose to stay out of sight during the day," he declares. "Sir Humphrey might be keeping watch! We don't want him to see us arrive."

As the pair near the farm, the Sage tells Rupert he will wait for him outside. "The less disturbance we make the better!" he declares. "Bring the golden goose back with you and we'll be able to take off in the Brella without being seen." Rupert crosses the silent farmyard and tip-toes to the hut where the geese all live. "Hello!" he whispers. "It's me, Rupert Bear! I've thought of somewhere safe for you to go. Come out and join me. We can set off while it's dark, so that nobody sees . . ."

RUPERT IS CAUGHT

*"I've come to take you far away
To somewhere where it's safe to stay!"*

*The goose agrees. "I thought those men
Might come and search the farm again . . ."*

*Scrogg blocks the way. "You don't fool me!
Is that a golden egg I see?"*

*He grabs the goose, and Rupert too,
"Sir Humphrey wants a word with you!"*

The golden goose is delighted with Rupert's plan. "Um Island sounds perfect!" it smiles. "Peace and quiet, no nosy visitors and with all those unicorns for company I'll certainly never be lonely!" Disappearing into the goose hut to say its farewells, it emerges with the golden egg and follows Rupert across the farmyard, to where the Sage is waiting . . . "I was so worried those men might come back!" the goose tells Rupert. "They didn't seem the type to give up easily!"

"Give up?" growls a deep voice. "Just as well we didn't, isn't it? Sir Humphrey said we'd find you sooner or later, and here you are - with a golden egg too! He *will* be pleased . . ." Before Rupert can stop him, the burly figure picks up the goose and calls to his companion. "Bring the bear as well!" orders Sir Humphrey. "We don't want him running off for help as soon as we're gone." Seizing Rupert by his jumper, Scrogg lifts him up and strides towards the waiting car.

The path's blocked by an angry flock
Of geese, which give Scrogg quite a shock!

"Quick!" Rupert urges. "Run while they
Stop Scrogg and let us get away!"

The Sage spots Rupert. "Goodness me!
We need to leave immediately . . ."

He hovers ready in mid-air,
"I'll save you from that pesky pair!"

Just as it seems that all is lost, a noisy honking sound makes Scrogg stop in his tracks. The next moment, Gertie and the other geese crowd around him, hissing and pecking angrily. "Stop that! Help!" cries Sir Humphrey's servant, flailing at the birds in alarm. "Come on!" Rupert whispers to the golden goose. "Now's our chance! Your friends will give us time to get away." "Scrogg!" calls Sir Humphrey. "Leave those silly geese and get after the one with the golden egg!"

"Come back here!" bellows Scrogg. "You won't get away that easily, you know!" By now Rupert has spotted the Sage of Um, who blinks with surprise, then hops into the waiting Brella. By the time Rupert reaches him, his friend is hovering in the air, poised for a quick escape . . . "Well done!" he calls. "Jump aboard and you'll soon be out of Sir Humphrey's reach." Rupert seizes his hand and clambers in. The goose follows, leaping into Rupert's arms as the Brella starts to rise.

RUPERT FLIES IN THE BRELLA

Scrogg tries to catch the goose but fails -
"They're flying out of reach!" he wails.

Sir Humphrey shakes his fist. "I'll get
That goose in my collection yet!"

"Don't worry! He won't capture you
And put you in a private zoo . . ."

"Look out!" cries Rupert. "Down below,
They're following us as we go!"

Scrogg makes a desperate lunge as the Brella takes off but it is too late . . . "Hold on tight!" calls the Sage. "Up we go!" Rupert and the goose peer down at Sir Humphrey and Scrogg, who stand gasping in the farmyard below. "Hurrah!" laughs Rupert. "We made it! You'll be safe now." "Don't be so sure!" calls Sir Humphrey, shaking his fist angrily. "Nobody makes a fool of me and gets away with it. I'll catch that goose if it's the last thing I do! Just you wait and see . . ."

"Sir Humphrey Pumphrey!" scoffs the Sage as the Brella flies away from Nutwood. "People like that are a real menace. The very thought of putting our friend here in a private zoo! I'm glad to say there's no danger of that happening now. He'll never find you on Um, no matter how much he huffs and puffs." Rupert looks back towards the farm and spots a fast car speeding along the road. "It's Sir Humphrey and Scrogg!" he gasps. "They must have decided to follow us . . ."

The Sage tells Rupert not to mind.
"We'll soon leave Pumphrey far behind!"

"Sir Humphrey has to stop, while we
Can fly on, out across the sea."

The car drives straight towards the shore
But just as quickly as before!

"Bless me!" the Sage blinks. "It can float -
Sir Humphrey's car's just like a boat!"

Although Sir Humphrey's car is very fast, the Sage of Um doesn't seem to be too bothered by the thought of being chased . . . "Look!" he laughs and points ahead. "The sea!" cries Rupert. "Of course! He won't be able to follow us now." "That's one of the main reasons I settled on Um!" says the Sage. "It's miles and miles from the mainland." They reach the coast and sail out across the sea, which glistens in the silvery moonlight. "Full speed ahead!" calls the Sage.

As the Brella flies out to sea, Rupert looks back towards Sir Humphrey. "He's still driving fast!" he calls. "They'll end up in the sea if they don't stop soon!" blinks the Sage. To the friends' astonishment, their pursuer shows no sign of slowing down but drives straight towards them, floating on the surface of the water! "An amphibious car!" marvels the Sage. "Sir Humphrey's more resourceful than I'd thought! We'll have to try to shake him off our trail!"

RUPERT REACHES UM ISLAND

"We'll have to hope Sir Humphrey's car
Finds travelling to Um too far . . ."

The Brella flies on through the night
And reaches Um as it grows light.

The Brella lands. "With luck we'll find
We've left Sir Humphrey's car behind!"

But then the goose points out to sea -
"Sir Humphrey!" gasps the Sage. "Dear me!"

"I'm afraid Sir Humphrey is trying to follow us!" says the Sage. "He knows we've got the golden goose and seems determined to catch it." "What if he reaches Um Island?" blinks Rupert. "The moment he sees the unicorns he'll try to capture them as well!" "You're right!" says the Sage."We'll just have to hope he doesn't get that far . . ." The Brella speeds on across the sea until the sky lightens and dawn begins to break. "Land ahoy!" calls Rupert. "It's Um Island!"

As soon as they reach Um the Brella swoops down to land on a grassy slope above the rocky shore. "So far so good!" says the Sage. "I only hope Sir Humphrey has given up the chase and turned back towards the mainland . . ." Just then, the golden goose squawks in alarm and points out to sea, towards a dark shape approaching on the horizon. "Sir Humphrey!" gasps Rupert. "He hasn't given up at all! He must have been following us all through the night . . ."

RUPERT PLANS A SURPRISE

The Sage sets off across the isle
But Rupert stops and starts to smile . . .

"The unicorns! Together we
Can stop Sir Humphrey yet - you'll see . . ."

The friends all hide away before
Sir Humphrey's car reaches the shore . . .

"Look!" Scrogg calls out excitedly.
"The goose! Sir Humphrey! Follow me . . ."

The Sage decides that the best place to hide the goose is in a cave near the middle of the island. "Follow me!" he says. "We need to get there before the others arrive." As they set off Rupert hears an excited whinny and spots a unicorn galloping towards them, together with a little foal. "Hello!" cries the Sage. "I've brought some visitors with me. This is Rupert Bear, from Nutwood." Rupert strokes the foal and suddenly thinks of a way to trick Sir Humphrey . . .

By the time Sir Humphrey reaches the island, Rupert and the others have hidden themselves away, just near the spot where they first landed. "Good!" says Rupert as the car drives on to the sand. "They've come ashore at exactly the right place." "Um Island!" laughs Sir Humphrey. "Those fools have led us straight to it. All we have to do now is track down that dratted goose." "It's there!" calls Scrogg excitedly, pointing along the beach. "Quick, Boss! Come and help me catch it!"

RUPERT HIDES FROM VIEW

The goose spots Scrogg and runs away.
Sir Humphrey tries to make it stay . . .

Then suddenly they spot a sight
That fills Sir Humphrey with delight.

"The foal, Scrogg! Look, it's got a horn!
At last, I've found a unicorn!"

Another unicorn appears.
"She's the foal's mother!" Pumphrey cheers.

As soon as it spots Scrogg the goose runs off, away from the beach towards the middle of the island. "Come back!" calls Sir Humphrey. "There's no need for alarm. Scrogg and I can offer you a home. A haven for rare creatures! Trust me I . . ." All of a sudden, he stops in his tracks and stares ahead in wonder. "A unicorn!" gasps Scrogg. "I don't believe it!" whispers Sir Humphrey. "Careful, Scrogg! We don't want to frighten it off . . ."

Sir Humphrey stares at the baby unicorn in wonder. "All my life I've dreamt of finding one!" he murmurs. "It's amazing! Simply amazing!" "What about the goose?" asks Scrogg. "Leave it!" snaps his companion. "*This* is the prize we want! Imagine owning the only unicorn in captivity . . ." As he speaks, the foal turns to a grassy clearing where a full-grown unicorn appears. "Another one!" gasps Scrogg. "She must be the mother!" blinks Sir Humphrey. "How delightful!"

RUPERT FOOLS SIR HUMPHREY

"More unicorns!" Sir Humphrey cries.
"We've found a herd Scrogg! What a prize!"

"These unicorns are wild and free!
Not yours!" calls Rupert angrily.

"Sir Humphrey has a private zoo!
He plans to try to capture you . . ."

"Run, boss!" calls Scrogg. "Those unicorns
Are dangerous. Look at their horns!"

To the zoo-owner's delight, more unicorns join the foal and its mother in the grassy clearing. "There's a whole herd!" he calls to Scrogg. "The last unicorns in the world, and they're ours for the taking . . ." "No they're not!" cries Rupert, suddenly emerging from his hiding place. "The unicorns are wild creatures which live here in peace. Nobody owns them, and nobody ever will!" "That's what you think!" glowers Sir Humphrey. "This time, nothing will stand in my way!"

To Sir Humphrey's surprise, Rupert is joined by more and more unicorns, who lower their horns menacingly. "They don't look very friendly!" gasps Scrogg. "These men threaten your island!" calls Rupert. "They tried to catch the golden goose and now they want to catch you too!" "Look out, boss!" calls Scrogg. "Run for your life!" The goose honks loudly and the unicorns begin to charge. "Back to the car!" cries Sir Humphrey. "Hurrah!" laughs Rupert. "Our plan's working . . ."

RUPERT SAVES THE GOLDEN GOOSE

The men keep running till they reach
The car they've left parked on the beach . . .

"Bravo!" laughs Rupert. "That was fun!
Sir Humphrey's given up! We've won!"

"Good!" laughs the Sage. "I don't think they
Will trouble us again today."

"I know the very place for you!
Where lots of other birds live too . . ."

Pursued by the unicorns, Sir Humphrey and Scrogg scramble down to the beach and race back towards their car. "They're getting closer!" wails Scrogg. "I can hear the thunder of hooves . . ." "Keep running!" puffs his chief. "There isn't much further to go!" The two men leap into the car and drive off without a backward glance. "Good riddance!" cheers Rupert as he watches them put to sea. The goose honks and the unicorns all neigh delightedly.

"Well done!" cries the Sage. "You gave Sir Humphrey and Scrogg such a fright they forgot all about our feathered friend . . ." The goose picks up Scrogg's cap and carries it off as a trophy. "Do you think they'll ever come back?" asks Rupert. "They might!" says the Sage, "Although I don't think they'll try to catch any more unicorns!" Turning to the goose, he declares that he's thought of an even better home for it than Um Island. "It's just the place for a special bird!"

RUPERT MEETS THE BIRD KING

The Brella flies across the sea -
Where can its destination be?

"A castle!" Rupert gives a cry -
"The Bird King's Palace in the sky!"

The Brella lands. A guard asks who
They are and what they've come to do . . .

"We've brought a bird for you to see.
It's very rare, Your Majesty!"

Rupert is mystified. "Where can be safer than Um Island?" he thinks. "Climb aboard the Brella and you'll soon find out!" smiles the Sage. "I'll take you there straightaway." The unicorns gather to bid farewell to Rupert as the Brella speeds out to sea. Climbing higher and higher, it emerges above the clouds in a haze of dazzling sunshine . . . Ahead of them, Rupert spots the turrets of a large castle. "The Bird King's Palace!" he cries. "I should have guessed! It's the perfect hideaway!"

As the Brella lands, an astonished guard comes hurrying to meet it. "Hello!" calls Rupert. "We've come from Um Island, with a special visitor to see your King . . ." The Bird King is told of Rupert's arrival and agrees to see him immediately. "A special visitor, Your Majesty!" declares the guard. "The Sage of Um?" asks the King. "No!" laughs Rupert. "The Sage and I have brought you a special *bird* to join your flock." "A bird!" blinks the King. "Let us see it straightaway!"

RUPERT SAYS GOODBYE

"A golden egg!" the Bird King cries,
Unable to believe his eyes . . .

The King says the gold eggs can be
Stored safely in his Treasury.

"I'll tell the other geese where you
Are living - they can visit too . . ."

"Just wait till Odmedod hears how
The goose has found a safe home now!"

The goose steps forward with a gleaming golden egg. "Can this be true?" gasps the King. "I have heard tell of such things in my grandfather's time, but I never dreamt of a golden goose gracing Our Court!" The King is so pleased that he puts the goose in charge of the Royal Treasury. "Your golden eggs will be stored in our strongroom, safe from all treasure-seekers!" he declares. "From now on, you will dwell among friends and enjoy the protection of the entire Palace Guard!"

Rupert and the Sage are delighted that the goose has found a proper home. "I'll tell Farmer Brown's geese where you are!" Rupert promises. The golden goose beams delightedly as the King thanks the pair for all they've done. "I'll take you back to Nutwood now!" smiles the Sage as he and Rupert leave in the Brella. "Thanks!" says Rupert. "Just wait till Odmedod hears everything that's happened!"

*The holidays have just begun -
Rupert and Algy plan some fun . . .*

*They pack their rucksacks full, then take
A two-man tent towards the lake.*

It is the beginning of the summer holidays. Rupert and Algy have been planning a boating trip together and are up bright and early, eager to start their expedition . . . "Have fun!" says Mrs. Bear as she bids the pair farewell. "I've packed some food you can cook for your supper, when you set up camp for the night." "Thank you," says Algy, "We'll be hungry after a day on the river. It's hard work, paddling along . . ."

The chums' tent folds into a large bundle, which they carry between them across the fields. "It's wonderful!" laughs Rupert. "I can hardly believe we're setting off at last . . ." "Me neither!" says Algy. "In perfect weather too! Warm sunshine and not a cloud in the sky . . ." "There's the lake!" calls Rupert. "Down to the water's edge, then along the path to the boathouse . . ." "Hurrah!" cheers Algy. "We'll soon be there!"

and the Raft

"This way!" says Algy as he sees
The boathouse in amongst the trees.

"Hurrah!" cries Rupert. "Here's our boat!
Let's clear her out and get afloat . . ."

Rupert and Algy carry their load along a grassy path by the edge of the lake. "Not much further now!" puffs Algy as he spots the boathouse in amongst the trees . . . The two chums often go boating together and share a favourite canoe, which is stored inside for the winter. "Do you remember our last trip?" asks Rupert. "When we went all the way to Nutchester!" "Yes!" nods Algy. "That was fun . . . but this will be even better."

"Here she is!" says Rupert, pulling aside a heavy tarpaulin to reveal the old canoe. "Just the same as when we left her! The paddles should be underneath, together with a mug for bailing out . . ." "I hope we won't be needing that very often!" says Algy. "I'll help you fold the sheet, then we'll see about getting her into the water . . . It's always exciting when we launch the boat. It seems like the real start of Summer!"

RUPERT AND ALGY GO BOATING

The two pals stow their tent below,
Then clamber in - all set to go . . .

They paddle off without delay -
"Good! Now we're really underway!"

"There's Bingo!" Algy calls. "What's he
So busy making now? Let's see . . ."

Their chum explains he wants to make
A raft to sail on Nutwood's lake.

Launching their boat into the water, Rupert and Algy paddle out of the boathouse and moor by the water's edge. "I'll put the tent in, together with our packs," says Rupert. "If we balance it in the middle, we'll hardly know it's there . . ." Clambering into the canoe, the pair start paddling and soon get into their stride. "Steady as she goes!" calls Algy. "Right you are!" laughs Rupert. "We'll keep going till we reach the mouth of the river. It shouldn't take long now we're underway."

As Rupert and Algy paddle along, they suddenly hear the sound of someone hammering. "It's Bingo!" cries Algy. "He's over there, on the far side! I wonder what he's up to?" The chums paddle across to see and find their inventor friend busy at work on a makeshift raft. "Hello!" he smiles. "I thought *I'd* try a spot of boating too. Actually, this is the *second* raft I've made. If I still had the first one we could have paddled upstream together . . ."

RUPERT HEARS BINGO'S TALE

"The first one I made looked just right
But then it vanished in the night!"

"The next day, all that I could find
Was this old rope it left behind . . ."

The pals tell Bingo they'll look out
For his raft, if it's still about.

They turn off from the lake and then
Resume their journey once again . . .

The chums moor their boat and climb ashore to talk to Bingo. "Why do you have to build a *second* raft?" asks Rupert. "Whatever happened to the first?" "I wish I knew!" sighs the brainy pup. "I left it here, tied to a tree one night, and when I came back, the next day, it had completely disappeared!" Bingo shows the others how the rope he used to tether the raft has snapped in half. "It must have been a storm!" he shrugs. "If the raft broke free then it might have drifted anywhere."

Leaving Bingo to get on with his work, Rupert and Algy climb back into their boat and set off once again. "We'll keep an eye open for your *first* raft!" promises Rupert. "Someone might have found it, floating on the lake . . ." The chums keep paddling until they reach a narrow turning, off the main lake. "This is the way!" calls Rupert. "We can paddle upstream towards the source!" "I'll look out for a good spot to pitch the tent," says Algy. "We don't want to leave it too late!"

RUPERT SETS UP CAMP

*"We need to find a camping site . . .
I think that grassy bank looks right."*

*"It's perfect!" Algy smiles. "Now we
Can pitch our tent and cook some tea."*

*He sets to work and soon the pair
Have supper in the open air.*

*"Let's check the map now, so we know
Exactly which way we should go."*

Paddling slowly along the stream, Rupert and Algy watch the sun sinking lower and lower, lighting the banks with a golden glow. "How about stopping there?" suggests Rupert. "Perfect!" says Algy. "We'll unpack the tent and set to work . . ." Rupert spreads the tent out carefully, then starts to fix the poles. "I hope I can remember how it goes!" he says. "It's a whole year since the last time I put up a tent." "Well done!" cheers Algy. "Now *I'll* cook some tea!"

Algy sets to work and soon has a pan of eggs and bacon sizzling on the fire. "Delicious!" says Rupert. "A day on the river gives you quite an appetite!" The chums sit talking till dark, then clamber into their sleeping bags. "Let's have a look at the map," suggests Rupert. "The river twists and turns so much, we ought to make sure we know the way." By the light of Algy's torch, the pair can see the whole of Nutwood's countryside, from familiar landmarks to far-off hills . . .

RUPERT IS WOKEN BY FROGS

Next morning, Rupert wakes to hear
A strange sound come from somewhere near . .

He peers outside the tent and blinks
"It's frogs! They're everywhere!" he thinks.

As Algy steps outside they all
Crowd round . . . More frogs take up the call!

Then, suddenly, the croaking ends -
A big frog comes towards the friends . . .

Early next morning, Rupert and Algy are woken by a strange noise. "What's that?" gasps Algy. "It's getting louder and louder!" Rupert listens carefully. "Some sort of animal!" he declares. "It must be very close . . ." Untying the flaps of the tent, Rupert peers out cautiously, then gives an astonished cry. "Frogs!" he gasps. "They're all round the tent. As they catch sight of Rupert the frogs start croaking louder then ever. "How odd!" he thinks. "I wonder what they want?"

"What a din!" cries Algy as he climbs out to join Rupert. "I've never seen so many frogs . . ." The chums' tent is completely surrounded by frogs of all sizes, who keep up a rowdy chorus of croaking, which gets even louder as more and more frogs arrive. All of a sudden, the noise stops as a large frog, wearing a sash, approaches. The others all turn to him as if waiting for some sort of proclamation. "Do you think he's their leader?" whispers Algy. "I wonder?" says Rupert.

RUPERT FOLLOWS A MESSENGER

*"Hello!" the frog declares. "I bring
An urgent summons from our King!"*

*"He needs your help. Please follow me.
I'll lead you to His Majesty . . ."*

*The pals set off along the shore
But can't guess where they're heading for . . .*

*"The King's Apartments are not far
But only frogs know where they are!"*

"Greetings!" calls the large frog. "The news from our scouts was true, I see. They said two campers had been spotted by the riverbank . . ." "I'm sorry if we're in the way," starts Rupert but the frog cuts him short with a laugh. "No, no! We were *glad* to see your tent. The Frog King has sent me to ask for help with a very urgent problem." "Frog King?" blinks Rupert. "Yes," says the messenger. "His Majesty is anxious to meet you. Follow me and I'll lead the way."

Rupert and Algy follow the messenger along a riverside path. "I didn't even know there *was* a Frog King!" whispers Algy. "I wonder what he wants us to do?" "I don't know," says Rupert. "This way!" calls the frog. "The King's Residence is quite nearby . . ." Rupert can't imagine where the Messenger Frog is taking them. "I've never seen a palace near the river," he murmurs. "Not many have!" smiles the frog. "The Royal Quarters are hidden away where only we can find them."

48

RUPERT MEETS THE FROG KING

As Rupert walks along he sees
A lily pond, fringed by tall trees.

"This way!" the frog calls. "We can take
The floating path across the lake . . ."

Although the two chums hesitate
The lily pads can bear their weight!

The willows part and now the pair
Can see the Frog King sitting there . . .

To Rupert's surprise, the Messenger leads them away from the main river, to a small pond, covered in water lilies. Tall trees grow all around, with weeping willows stretching down to the water's edge. "Follow me closely!" orders the frog. "Tread exactly where I walk . . ." As the chums look on, he steps on to a lily pad and begins to walk calmly across the pond. "We can't do that!" gasps Algy. "They'll never support our weight!" "Let's try," says Rupert. "Perhaps they're a special kind . . ."

To Rupert and Algy's surprise, the lily pads hold their weight with ease. "They're just like stepping stones!" laughs Algy. The Messenger sets off across the pond towards a huge willow, which reaches right down to the surface of the water. Pushing through a leafy curtain, he gestures for Rupert and Algy to follow . . . "The King!" gasps Algy. On the far side of the lake, Rupert spots a regal figure, wearing a golden crown. The Messenger croaks a greeting, then points to the approaching pair.

RUPERT HEARS ABOUT THE RIVER

*The Frog King greets his guests. "Thank you
For coming when I asked you to . . ."*

*"I need your help to find out why
The source of Nutwood's lake's run dry!"*

*"This marker pole is how we know
The water level's falling low . . ."*

*"It's got so bad I fear that we
Are faced with a catastrophe!"*

The Frog King peers at the chums, then nods
for them to step ashore. "Welcome!" he booms.
"You come from Nutwood, I assume?" "That's
right, Your Majesty," says Rupert. "We're on a
boating trip along the river." "Excellent!" smiles
the frog. "Sorry to interrupt your journey, but
there's a threat to Nutwood Lake that frogs alone
can't overcome." "A threat?" gasps Rupert.
"What's wrong?" "It's drying up!" declares the
King. "The level's sinking lower and lower . . ."

"The water level's been falling for days!" declares
the King. "We measure it with this marker pole!"
The Messenger Frog explains why the drop is so
serious. "It's not *just* this pond that's fallen," he
croaks. "Nutwood Lake's the same! They're all
joined by a system of rivers and streams . . ." "We
didn't *see* anything wrong," says Rupert. "You
wouldn't!" says the frog. "That's why we use a
marker. By the time folk start to notice it's too late.
We need early warning while there's still time!"

RUPERT PROMISES TO HELP

The two pals tell the King that they
Will find out what's wrong straightaway.

The frogs who guide the chums all seem
To think the problem lies upstream . . .

With every step the level sinks -
"It's getting lower!" Algy blinks.

"The water has a single source
From which the river runs its course . . ."

The Frog King tells Rupert and Algy that nobody knows why the water level is falling. "That's why we need your help," he explains. "Unless the mystery's solved soon the ponds and rivers will start to dry up . . ." "That would be terrible!" says Rupert. "There must be something causing the drop, it's just a question of finding what's wrong . . ." The pair decide to start by following the river back to its source. "This way!" says the Messenger Frog. "Follow me . . ."

Following the Messenger Frog along the banks of the river, Rupert and Algy are shocked to see how low the water has fallen. "It seems to be getting worse!" gasps Algy. "Yes!" nods the frog. "I can't remember it being this *low*, even in last year's drought, when it didn't rain for weeks and weeks." The Messenger explains that the whole river system is fed by a single spring. "We should reach it soon," he croaks. "All we have to do is follow the course of the river as far as we can . . ."

*"A torrent used to fill this bed -
Now just a trickle flows instead!"*

*Ahead of them, the two pals see
An obstacle - what can it be?*

*"A gate!" cries Algy. "Somebody
Has blocked the flow deliberately!"*

*"It looks more like a capsized craft!"
The Messenger declares. "A raft?"*

The Messenger Frog tells the chums that when the river is flowing in full spate the sound of the water is deafening. "It's only a trickle now!" thinks Rupert. "No wonder the level of Nutwood Lake has fallen!" Rounding a bend the frog stares into the distance, then groans in dismay. "That's where the spring starts!" he explains. "It should be much higher than that . . ." "The river must be blocked!" says Rupert. "You're right!" says Algy. "I'm sure I can see something lying in the water . . ."

As the chums get nearer, they can see that the river is blocked by what looks like some sort of gate . . . "It's an old door!" cries Algy. "Someone's cut the water off deliberately!" At first Rupert thinks that his chum must be right, but as he looks more carefully, he realises what they've found . . . "It's a raft!" blinks the Messenger. "Most unusual to be this far upstream!" "It must have capsized," says Rupert. "The rocks are holding it fast and the water can't get through."

RUPERT UNBLOCKS THE STREAM

"It's Bingo's!" Rupert cries. "I'm sure -
The lost raft that he made before!"

"The mystery's over! Now we know
Why Nutwood's river's ceased to flow . . ."

The two pals lift the raft which blocks
The dammed up river from the rocks.

The frog lets out a joyful cry
To see the water rushing by . . .

The Messenger Frog is mystified by the abandoned raft, but Rupert suddenly realises where it must have come from. "It's Bingo's!" he cries. "The *first* raft he built. The one that was carried away in a storm . . ." Now the chums have discovered what's wrong, all that remains is for them to try to clear the river. "It won't be easy!" warns the frog. "Let's try!" Rupert tells Algy. "I'll cross over while you stay there." Taking a giant leap he hops across, landing safely on the far side.

As the Messenger looks on, Rupert and Algy take hold of the upturned raft. "Let's see if we can lift it clear," says Rupert. At first it seems impossible to shift but as the chums pull together it suddenly starts to move. "That's got it free of the rocks," calls Rupert. "Now let's try to unblock the stream . . ." The pair haul the raft out to the bank then peer down at the river, which rushes past in a sudden swell. "Hurrah!" cheers the Messenger. "Nutwood Lake is saved!"

RUPERT AND ALGY SET SAIL

"Let's see if Bingo's raft will take
Us back downstream to Nutwood's lake . . ."

"We're off now! Hold tight everyone!"
Calls Algy to the frogs. "What fun!"

The pals' plan works - soon they can see
The Frog King's mighty willow tree . . .

"The river's back to normal now!
You two have saved the day - but how?"

As they watch the river racing past, Rupert and Algy decide to use the abandoned raft to ride back to Nutwood . . . "There's plenty of room!" says Rupert, as he climbs aboard. The Messenger seems doubtful at first, but is soon persuaded by the other frogs, who are keen to have a ride. Algy holds the raft steady until everyone is ready, then jumps across to join Rupert. "Hold tight!" he calls. "We're off!" The raft gives a sudden lurch, then starts to speed downstream . . .

To Rupert's delight, the chums' plan works splendidly. The raft whizzes down the fast-flowing stream towards the frogs' special pond. "I can see the big willow!" calls Algy excitedly. "I wonder if the King's still there?" says Rupert. Although the raft has started to slow down, it still glides silently across the pond towards the curtain of leaves. As the chums push their way through, the Frog King looks up and blinks with astonishment to see that they are back so soon.

Rupert and the Raft

RUPERT IS THANKED BY THE KING

The Frog King marvels as he hears
The two pals' tale. "Well done!" he cheers.

He thanks the chums, "Without you two
We'd never have known what to do!"

The frogs all gather round and say
They'll help the pals' raft on its way . . .

Before long, Algy spots the place
Where they turned off from the main race.

"Bravo!" cheers the King when he hears how the chums cleared the river. "I saw the water start to rise but couldn't imagine what you'd done . . ." He looks at the raft and seems astonished that it made the journey all the way downstream. "An excellent way of travelling," enthuses the Messenger. "Perhaps we should have one for special expeditions!" laughs the King. "Thank you again for helping us solve the mystery," he tells Rupert. "We'd never have done it without you!"

Now that Nutwood Lake is back to normal, Rupert and Algy decide to return to their camp. "I wonder if we can sail back?" asks Algy. "We might," says Rupert, "but it won't be easy . . ." "Don't worry!" laughs the Frog King. "Climb aboard and leave the rest to us!" The chums step on to the raft and are immediately surrounded by a crowd of frogs, who offer to push them along. "You'll be there in no time!" calls the King. "Wonderful!" smiles Algy as the raft glides along.

55

RUPERT HEARS A CALL

The raft drifts on downstream and then
The two pals spot their tent again . . .

They thank the frogs and jump ashore -
Delighted to be back once more.

"Look!" Algy gives a startled cry -
The chums spot Bingo floating by . . .

"You've found my raft!" he blinks. "But where . . ."
"It's quite a story!" laugh the pair.

Following the course of the stream, Rupert and Algy soon spot their tent, half-hidden amongst the trees. "Our boat's still there too," says Rupert. "Let's try to moor the raft in the same spot." The frogs keep pushing until the chums reach the bank, then hop ashore for a final farewell. "It's our turn to thank *you* now," smiles Rupert. "We couldn't have had a better boating trip . . ." "I'll say!" laughs Algy as he ties up the raft. "Even though we left our boat behind."

Rupert and Algy are about to settle down to have breakfast when they suddenly spot another raft, travelling upstream. "Bingo!" calls Algy. "You'll never guess what we've found! Come and see . . ." The brainy pup can hardly believe his eyes when he spots the missing raft. "Amazing!" he blinks. "I thought it had gone forever!" "Wait till you hear the whole story!" laughs Rupert. "We'll tell you about it, over breakfast . . ."

RUPERT

and the Sundial

John Harrold.

RUPERT FEELS HOT

A long hot summer pleases some,
But Rupert's dad wants rain to come . . .

Mrs. Bear says, "Don't be dismayed!
I'll make us all some lemonade . . ."

Bill Badger's mother stops to say,
***"Another** lovely sunny day . . ."*

"We're out of lemons, I'm afraid!"
Says Mr. Chimp. "Try orangeade!"

It has been a long, hot summer in Nutwood, with the sun blazing down every day . . . "This can't go on much longer!" complains Mr. Bear. "If it doesn't rain soon the garden will be ruined! The lawn looks parched, the roses are over and everything else is wilting." "It is rather hot!" agrees Mrs. Bear. "I think we could all do with a nice cool drink! How about some lemonade?" "Yes, please!" says Rupert. "Coming up!" smiles Mrs. Bear. "I'll just go and buy some lemons . . ."

Rupert decides to go with his mother to the shops. On the way there, the pair meet Bill and Mrs. Badger. "Hello!" she smiles. "Isn't this heatwave lovely? I can't remember when it last rained!" "Me neither!" laughs Mrs. Bear. When they reach the village shop, Rupert and his mother see that they are not the only ones to think of making lemonade . . . "Sold out of lemons, I'm afraid!" says Mr. Chimp. "These little oranges are all I'll have now, until next week's delivery."

RUPERT MEETS PODGY PIG

"I'll go this way, if you don't mind,
There might be some pals I can find . . ."

"There's Podgy Pig! He's playing catch -
Perhaps he'd like a football match?"

"Hello!" calls Podgy. "Look at me!
I've learnt to juggle! Come and see . . ."

"It's fun with fruit!" says Podgy. "You
Can juggle some, then eat it too!"

As Mrs. Bear returns with a bag of oranges, Rupert decides to take a longer path across the common to see if he can spot any of his chums. "See you later!" calls his mother. "Don't get too hot in the sun!" Rupert hasn't gone far when he spots his pal, Podgy, playing with an orange ball. "I wonder what he's up to?" he thinks. "Now it's a *yellow* ball he's got . . ." Full of curiosity, Rupert hurries across the common towards his chum, who seems to be completely engrossed . . .

As Rupert gets nearer, he sees that Podgy is busy juggling . . . "Those aren't balls!" he gasps. "They're oranges and lemons!" "Hello!" smiles Podgy. "You didn't know I could do this, did you?" "No!" admits Rupert. "Neither did I!" laughs his chum. "I had to practise for ages before I got it right!" Podgy stops juggling and starts to peel one of the enormous oranges. "Time for another snack!" he declares. "They're really delicious. Try a piece and see for yourself . . ."

RUPERT IS GIVEN AN ORANGE

*"Delicious!" Rupert cries. "But all
The oranges we saw were small . . ."*

*"Not these!" laughs Podgy gleefully.
"I picked them myself - from the tree!"*

*"Have one!" says Podgy. "I know where
To find so much, I've fruit to spare!"*

*"How odd!" thinks Rupert. "Is it true?
I wonder where this orange grew?"*

"You're right!" says Rupert as he bites into the orange. "It's juicier than the ones we normally get . . ." "Bigger too!" nods Podgy. "I could only fit six in my basket!" "Wherever did they come from?" asks Rupert. "Mr. Chimp's sold out!" "I know!" chuckles Podgy. "But these aren't from a shop. I picked them myself, straight from the tree . . ." "Picked them?" marvels Rupert. "Where?" "That would be telling!" smiles Podgy. "If everyone finds out, they'll all disappear!"

No matter how much Rupert asks him, Podgy refuses to say another word about where he found the oranges. "You can have one from my basket to take home," he declares. "But the tree's a secret. Only I know where it is - and that's how it's going to stay!" Rupert stares at the orange as Podgy marches away. "I can't believe it grew in Nutwood!" he gasps. "Perhaps Podgy got Tigerlily to conjure some up? Or perhaps he went for a ride in Pong-Ping's lift? I wonder if oranges grow in China?"

RUPERT SEES AN OLD PICTURE

"Look, Dad!" cries Rupert. "Do you know
Where oranges like this one grow?"

"In Nutwood?" murmurs Mr. Bear.
"The weather's too cold for them here!"

*"You **can** grow oranges on trees*
In special glasshouses - like these . . ."

"That house is one I recognise -
It's Nutwood Manor!" Rupert cries.

When Rupert gets home his parents are trying the orangeade . . . "This is all I could manage!" says Mrs. Bear. "We really need bigger oranges." "How's this?" says Rupert, producing Podgy's gift. "That's more like it!" nods his father. "But hasn't Mr. Chimp sold out?" When Rupert explains how Podgy picked the orange from a tree, his parents are astonished. "That's very unusual in England!" says Mr. Bear. "They grow in special glasshouses. There's a picture of one in this book."

"England's too cold for oranges," explains Mr. Bear. "They prefer hot countries like Spain and Morocco, or the warmth of a glasshouse - like this one . . ." Rupert looks carefully at the picture in his father's book. "They were quite popular, once," continues Mr. Bear. "Lots of big houses had orangeries." Rupert stares at the picture. "It looks just like Ottoline's house!" he gasps. Mr. Bear looks at the picture's caption. "Nutwood Manor!" he reads. "Goodness, Rupert! You're right."

RUPERT VISITS OTTOLINE

Rupert sets out to see if he
Can find the secret orange tree . . .

"Hello, Rupert!" calls Ottoline.
"I can't believe how hot it's been!"

*"We **had** a glasshouse, years ago,*
But now there's nothing much to show . . ."

"I'd like to put it right again -
One day perhaps - I don't know when!"

As soon as he finishes lunch, Rupert decides to visit Ottoline to look at Nutwood Manor's orangery . . . "I expect it's *full* of oranges and lemons!" he smiles. "Ottoline probably gave Podgy a basket for helping her gather fruit . . ." When he arrives, Rupert finds his chum out in the garden, reading a book. "Isn't this sunshine lovely?" she smiles. "I've never known a summer last so long!" "Hello!" calls Rupert. "I've come to see if you can help me solve a mystery . . ."

When Ottoline hears about Podgy's oranges, she smiles and shakes her head. "They didn't come from *here*, I'm afraid. The orangery is abandoned. Nobody has grown fruit in it for years . . ." As the pair cross the garden, Rupert recognises the same glasshouse he saw in Mr. Bear's book, but all broken and tumbling down . . . "I've always wanted to grow our own fruit," says Ottoline. "But Father says the orangery would cost too much to repair. It seems such a shame to leave it standing empty!"

RUPERT IS WOKEN BY AN ELF

"Good luck!" calls Ottoline. "Be sure
To tell me if you find out more!"

That night, Rupert tells Mrs. Bear
He'd like some cooling evening air.

As Rupert sleeps, he's woken by
The sound of someone's urgent cry . . .

An Autumn Elf! "I've come to see
If you can solve a mystery!"

"Let me know if you find out any more!" calls Ottoline as Rupert sets off home. "It's exciting to think of someone growing oranges in Nutwood, though I can't think who it can be . . ." Rupert's parents can't think where the oranges have come from either. "If Podgy said he picked them, then he probably did!" says Mrs. Bear. "Ask him again tomorrow." That night it is so hot that Rupert decides to sleep with his window open. "Just a little," he says. "The cool air feels delicious!"

As Rupert sleeps, he is suddenly woken by a noise at the open window . . . "Somebody's calling my name!" he thinks. "I wonder who it can be?" Sitting up in bed, he sees a shadowy figure clambering over the sill . . . "An Autumn Elf!" gasps Rupert as he recognises the little man. "Hello!" says the visitor. "Sorry to startle you, but I've been sent by the Chief Elf to ask for your help. There's something very strange going on in Nutwood. Very strange indeed . . ."

*"This summer there's been so much sun
The plants look as though Autumn's come!"*

*"Please help us, Rupert. Find out what
Has made the weather grow so hot!"*

*Next morning Mr. Bear says, "Strange!
The dial still points to sun! No change . . ."*

*"The Weather Clerk should sort things out -
Or else there'll be a Nutwood drought!"*

The Elf tells Rupert that Nutwood's summer heatwave is threatening to kill off next year's plants. "Everything's happening too quickly!" he complains. "Trees are shedding their leaves, flowers are dropping their petals and the grass is all scorched and dry." "Just what my father said!" nods Rupert. "It hasn't rained all summer . . ." "The Chief's stumped!" says the Elf. "Can *you* help us find out what's happening?" "I'll try!" promises Rupert. "Tell your Chief I'll do my best!"

Next morning, Rupert comes downstairs to find his father peering at the barometer. "*Still* no change!" he sighs. "I can't understand it! There isn't a drought in other parts of the county . . . Nutchester's just had two inches of rain! I suppose the Clerk of the Weather knows his job, but if we don't get a downpour soon, Nutwood will be a desert!" "The Clerk of the Weather!" thinks Rupert. "Of course! He's the person to sort things out. I'll send him a message straightaway . . ."

RUPERT SENDS A MESSAGE

"I'll ask the Clerk to send rain soon . . .
Just what I need - a big balloon!"

"I hope that the Weather Clerk sees,"
Thinks Rupert as he writes, "Help, Please!"

On Nutwood common, Rupert blows
The balloon till his message shows . . .

"It's working!" Rupert cries, "Hurray!"
A wind whisks the balloon away . . .

The Clerk is a kindly old man who controls the world's weather from an astonishing headquarters, up above the clouds. Rupert has met him before and is sure he will agree to help. "How can I send him a message?" he murmurs. Rummaging through his toy cupboard, he suddenly has an idea . . . "A balloon!" he cries. "I'll write a message on it, then send it up to where the Weather Clerk is bound to see!" Holding the balloon flat, he begins to write, "Weather Clerk - I need your help . . ."

As soon as the ink is dry, Rupert hurries out to the common and starts to blow up the balloon. To his delight, the writing on it grows bigger and bigger, until he is sure the Clerk will be able to read it easily. "Now all I need is a wind!" he thinks. Luckily, a breeze catches the balloon and carries it up into the sky. Rupert watches it drift higher and higher until it disappears into the clouds. "I'll wait here," he thinks. "Perhaps the Clerk will send a message back."

RUPERT MEETS THE WEATHER CLERK

As Rupert waits, a plane appears -
"The Weather Clerk's arrived!" he cheers.

"Hello!" the Clerk says. "I could read
Your message. Tell me what you need . . ."

The Clerk's amazed. "Nutwood's too dry?
You've had a drought? I can't think why . . ."

"I sent you rain clouds, let me see . . .
It should have rained quite recently!"

As Rupert waits on the common, he suddenly hears the drone of an engine. Looking up, he spots the Weather Clerk's cloud-hopper, swooping down towards him. "Hello!" calls the old man. "I got your message! Saw a red balloon drifting up through the clouds, then read what it said through my strongest telescope . . ." "Thank goodness!" says Rupert. "We really need your help! Everyone in Nutwood has been complaining about too much sunshine and how we haven't had a drop of rain . . ."

The Weather Clerk is astonished by Rupert's news. "Too much sunshine?" he blinks. "I've had complaints about too much *rain* before, but most people like the sun." "People don't mind, it's Nutwood's plants that need water!" explains Rupert. "If it doesn't rain soon they'll all wither and die!" "But I sent rain to Nutwood!" says the Clerk. "Last week! You should have had a wet weekend." "Not a dark cloud in the sky!" says Rupert. "It's been sunny for weeks and weeks . . ."

Rupert and the Sundial

RUPERT SEES PODGY AGAIN

The Clerk agrees to send more rain
Then flies off quickly in his plane . . .

Next moment, Rupert hears a call -
"Hello there! Any news at all?"

Rupert tells Ottoline that they
Should have rain soon, "It's on the way!"

"There's Podgy!" Rupert says. "Let's see
If he'll show us the orange tree . . ."

The Weather Clerk makes a note of Rupert's complaint and promises to send more rain to Nutwood at once. "I can't think what can have happened to your first batch of clouds!" he says. "It's very unusual for them to be blown so far off course . . ." No sooner has the Clerk left than Rupert hears a familiar call from the other side of the common. "Ottoline!" he cries. "Just wait till I tell you what's happened . . ." "More news?" asks his chum. "Don't say you've discovered Podgy's tree?"

Rupert tells Ottoline how he has been trying to help the Autumn Elves . . . "They're worried that this heatwave will kill off Nutwood's plants!" he explains. "Oh, dear!" says Ottoline. "I suppose they need a good, long spell of rain." "Exactly!" says Rupert. "I asked the Weather Clerk and he promised to send some straightaway." Just then, the chums spot Podgy, walking across the common with an empty basket. "Look!" says Rupert. "I wonder if he's off to gather more oranges?"

RUPERT FOLLOWS HIS CHUM

"More oranges?" laughs Podgy. "No!
I'm off to find where brambles grow . . ."

"I wonder?" Rupert says. "There's more
To this than meets the eye, I'm sure!"

The pair see where their chum's goal lies -
"The Professor's tower!" Rupert cries.

Then, suddenly, dark clouds appear.
"Hurray! At last we'll have rain here!"

Overcome with curiosity, Rupert asks his chum if he is off to pick more fruit . . . "More fruit?" laughs Podgy nervously. "Oh, oranges, you mean? There's not much chance of that! I suppose I *might* find some early blackberries, if I'm lucky. Bit of a wild goose chase really, but at least I'll have a good walk . . ." "How odd!" says Ottoline. "I didn't think Podgy liked walking!" "He doesn't!" smiles Rupert. "There's more to this than meets the eye! Let's follow him and see where he goes . . ."

To the chums' surprise, Podgy doesn't go far across the common, but turns off, towards the old Professor's tower . . . "I wonder what he's up to?" murmurs Rupert. "His basket's still empty, but I'm sure there aren't any fruit trees growing here!" As the pair follow Podgy, the sky above them suddenly grows darker and darker. "Rain clouds!" cries Ottoline. "Thank goodness!" cheers Rupert. "They must be from the Clerk of the Weather. He promised to put an end to Nutwood's drought."

RUPERT IS MYSTIFIED

"Help!" Ottoline cries. "We'll both be
Wet through! Let's shelter near this tree . . ."

But, as the two pals watch the sky,
The clouds veer off - "I wonder why?"

"How odd!" says Rupert. "Not a drop!
But why? It seems the sun won't stop . . ."

The pair meet Bodkin, "Come this way -
Free oranges for all today!"

The clouds above Nutwood look so dark and threatening that Rupert and Ottoline decide to take shelter. "There's going to be an absolute deluge!" says Ottoline. "We'll be lucky not to get soaked . . ." To the friends' surprise, the sky suddenly starts to clear as the rain clouds veer away from the Professor's tower. "They're moving off to Nutchester!" gasps Rupert. "I'm sure it's got something to do with the Professor. Let's go and see what he makes of this strange weather."

By the time that Rupert and Ottoline near the Professor's tower, the sky is completely clear again. "It's sunnier than ever!" shrugs Ottoline. "And we didn't have a drop of rain . . ." On the way into the garden, the pair meet the Professor's servant, Bodkin. "Hello!" he smiles. "Come in search of oranges? I asked Podgy to tell everyone in Nutwood to come and help themselves." "Oranges?" blinks Rupert. "Yes!" beams Bodkin proudly. "Plenty for all! Lots of lemons too!"

In Bodkin's garden Rupert sees
A grove of laden orange trees . . .

*"So **this** is Podgy's secret store!"*
Laughs Rupert. "Look! He's picking more!"

The pals hear the Professor call,
"Please help yourselves - there's fruit for all!"

The proud inventor says he'll show
The chums what helped the trees to grow . . .

Bodkin leads the mystified pals to a walled garden where a large sign reads, "Free oranges and lemons - please pick your own!" "Goodness!" blinks Rupert. "There isn't just *one* orange tree. There must be over twenty." "Twenty two, if you count the lemons," smiles Bodkin. "It's been one of our most successful experiments! The only thing I can't understand is why we haven't had more visitors . . ." "I can!" says Rupert, spotting a familiar-looking figure in amongst the trees.

"I was going to tell you about the oranges, really . . ." says Podgy. "Even *I* couldn't eat all these!" "I should hope not!" beams the Professor as he joins the pals in the garden. "Plenty of oranges for everyone! It's a bumper crop!" "I'll say!" agrees Rupert. "But *how* did you manage to grow so many? I thought England was too cold and rainy for oranges and lemons?" "It is, normally!" laughs the Professor. "That's why I made my new invention. Come and see!"

RUPERT SEES A NEW INVENTION

The pals climb up, then reach a door
All wondering what lies in store . . .

"My new machine! It's guaranteed
To bring the sunshine fruit trees need!"

"My sundial sends the clouds away
And gives us sunshine every day . . ."

"I see!" gasps Rupert. "Now it's plain
Why Nutchester's had so much rain!"

Rupert is always fascinated by the Professor's inventions and can hardly wait to see his latest device. To his surprise, they go past the main laboratory and up a flight of steps that leads to the roof of the tower. "Here we are!" puffs the Professor. "Guaranteed sunshine for oranges and lemons. Just the weather they like!" "W . . . what is it?" asks Ottoline, staring at the strange machine. "A sundial!" says the Professor. "It's been switched on all summer . . ."

To the chums' amazement, the Professor tells them that his latest invention increases the amount of sunshine by driving off clouds . . . "You just set the dial to show how much sun you want!" he explains. "I've chosen *very* hot, to help the oranges ripen." "That's what we saw!" cries Rupert. "Those clouds over Nutchester veered away just as we arrived." "Quite so!" says the Professor. "*They* get an extra shower of rain while it stays nice and sunny here in Nutwood."

RUPERT SOLVES THE MYSTERY

*"Your sundial's made Nutwood too dry -
Without rain, all our plants will die!"*

*"Oh, dear! I didn't realise!
You're quite right!" The Professor sighs.*

*"I'll turn the sundial off, but then
We won't have oranges again . . ."*

*"Wait!" Rupert cries. "I think I know
The perfect place where they can grow!"*

At last, Rupert knows why Nutwood has been having such a long, hot summer . . . "Your sundial has upset everything!" he tells the Professor. "Oranges like it this hot, but everything else in Nutwood has been wilting in a drought! No wonder the Clerk of the Weather was so puzzled! He kept sending rain clouds to Nutwood, but the moment they got here, your new invention drove them all away!" "Oh, dear!" gasps the Professor. "I never really thought about other plants . . ."

"What a shame!" says the Professor as he switches off the sundial. "I suppose I should have known better than to meddle with the weather! Nutwood just isn't sunny enough for oranges." "I wonder?" murmurs Rupert. "There is *one* place in Nutwood where your trees might grow . . ." The Professor listens carefully as Rupert tells him all about the ruined orangery at Nutwood Manor. "A splendid idea!" he smiles. "If Ottoline's parents agree, we'll start the repair work straightaway!"

RUPERT SAVES THE ORANGE TREES

The pals help Bodkin make repairs
"It's good as new now!" he declares.

The old Professor brings the trees –
"You've found the perfect home for these!"

Ottoline's mother's thrilled to see
The newly-filled orangery . . .

*"This time we'll share and **everyone***
Can come and join us in the fun!"

When Bodkin sees the old orangery, he tells the chums that all it needs is a good clean and some fresh panes of glass . . . "It's a wonderful building!" he declares. "In the old days, it must have been full of fruit for the big house!" When everything is ready, the Professor ferries all his trees to Ottoline's house on the back of a large lorry. "My word!" he marvels. "You *have* done well! This is just the place to put them. Light and airy, yet nice and warm . . ."

When the last of the Professor's trees have been carried inside, Ottoline fetches her mother to come and see . . . "How wonderful!" she cries. "It's a *real* orangery again!" This time, *all* Rupert's chums are invited to come and pick oranges and lemons. "There are plenty for everyone!" laughs Ottoline. "Good!" says Podgy. "Then that must mean me as well!" "Of course!" says Rupert. "You did discover the first tree, after all!"

Make Your Own Butterfly Cakes

Follow this recipe carefully (ask an adult to help you with the oven) and you can make your very own batch of butterfly cakes. They may not fly, but they should taste delicious ...

INGREDIENTS:
(makes 12 cakes)

4oz (113g) butter or margarine
4oz (113g) caster sugar
2 eggs
4oz (113g) self-raising flour
A pinch of salt
Butter cream *(for the topping–see below)*
Icing sugar

INSTRUCTIONS:

1. Pre-heat oven to 375 degrees F (Gas mark 5)

2. Grease a bun tray with butter or margarine (or line with individual paper cases).

3. Beat the butter in a bowl with a wooden spoon until it is soft. Add the caster sugar and keep stirring until the mixture is light and fluffy.

4. Crack the eggs into a separate bowl and beat thoroughly.

5. Add beaten eggs to the mixture a little at a time, then, using a metal spoon, gradually fold in the sifted flour and salt. Beat until final mixture is soft and creamy.

6. Use a spoon to half-fill each mould or paper case.

7. Bake in a pre-heated oven at 375 degrees F (Gas Mark 5) for 15-20 minutes, until cakes are golden and well-risen. Allow cakes to cool on a wire rack.

TO MAKE BUTTER-CREAM:

INGREDIENTS:

4oz (113g) icing sugar
2-3 drops of vanilla essence
1-2 tablespoons of milk

a. Beat softened butter until creamy

b. Gradually add sifted icing sugar and a few drops of vanilla essence.

c. Add enough milk to ensure a creamy texture. (You can use 2 tablespoons of freshly squeezed orange juice instead of the vanilla essence and milk if you prefer a different flavour).

---

8. When the cakes have cooled, slice off the top of each one and spoon on a little butter cream.

9. Cut the original top of each cake in half and stand these in the buttercream, like the wings of a butterfly.

10. Lightly dust the cakes with icing sugar. Now eat them before they fly away . . .

These two pictures look identical, but there are ten differences between them. Can you spot them all? *Answers on page 109*

Odd One Out

Look carefully at these drawings of Ottoline, Bill Badger and Pong-Ping.
Sort them into matching pairs and put a circle round the odd ones out.

76

Rupert's Crossword Puzzle

See if you can complete this crossword. Most of the answers can be found
in stories from this year's annual...

Across

1. One of the Fox brothers (5)
2. Useful note to take shopping (4)
4. Rupert's elephant chum (6)
5. Familiar village (7)
9. Sinister Count (7)
11. Professor's servant (6)
12. Opposite to hot (4)
13. Nutwood's young inventor (5)
14. Ice house, lived in by 10 down (5)
16. Not dry (3)
17. Rupert's cousin (4)
18. Frozen water (3)
19. No longer shut (4)
21. Town full of bakers (9)
22. Floating platform, made by 13 across (4)
24. Wooden figures- made to be knocked over (8)
27. Mr. _____, Nutwood's farmer (5)
28. Rupert's surname (4)
29. Works for 27 across. One of Rupert's most
    unusual chums (7)
30. Apply heat to 18 across (4)
32. Rupert's wise old friend, with a flying Brella.
    (4,2,2)
34. Millie is one of these. So is Mollie. (5)
35. ____ Pug. Another of Rupert's chums (4)
36. Worn by a king (5)
37. Winter sport, played by 10 down. (7)

Down

1. Another Fox brother. Identical to 1 across (6)
3. Summer warmer- good for oranges! (3)
6. Rare creature- lives on Um Island.
   Famous for its horn. (7)
7. Rupert's friend from Nutwood Manor (8)
8. October 31st- A night for frights! (9)
10. Rupert's relative from the Far North (5,5)
15. Sweet citrus fruit (6)
17. First month of the year (7)
20. Rupert's small friend (with a long tail!) (6,5)
23. The Bird King is one of these (6)
24. Silent birdscarer (9)
25. Temporary Nutwood dweller, collected
    by Jack Frost (7)
26. Directed by a Clerk. Predicted by Mr. Bear's
    barometer. (7)
31. Another citrus fruit. Less sweet than
    15 down (5)
33. Type of egg sought by Humphrey Pumphrey (4)

Solution on page 109

77

A PAGE TO COLOUR

Try to colour these two pictures as carefully as you can.

Which Story?

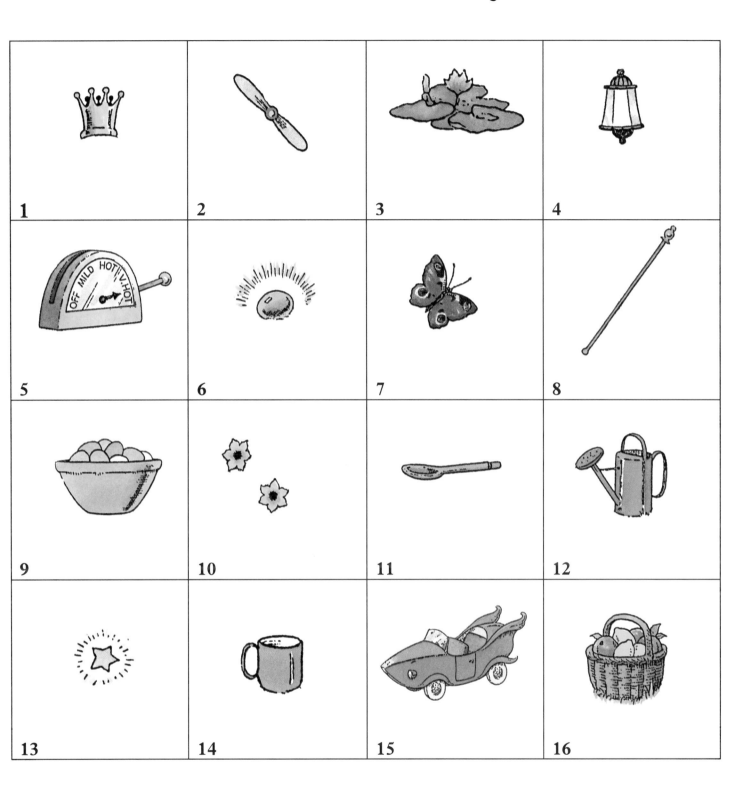

Each of the objects shown above appears in a story from this year's Annual.
Can you find where they are from?

Answers on page 109

RUPERT and

The post arrives one autumn day -
"An envelope - what does it say?"

One autumn morning, Rupert has just finished breakfast when he hears the post arrive . . . "It's an invitation!" he cries. "Ottoline's having a Halloween party and everyone is invited to come in fancy dress." "What fun!" says Rupert's father. "I remember bobbing for apples when I was a lad! We used to have lanterns too!" he chuckles. "You can make one if you like and take it to Ottoline's party to light the way . . ."

the Pumpkin Pie

"To Rupert Bear - from Ottoline!
Please join us all on Halloween . . ."

"A pumpkin lantern would be fun!"
Says Mr. Bear. "I'll buy you one . . ."

Rupert is so keen to make a lantern that his father agrees they can go and buy a pumpkin straightaway. "I saw a big pile in Mr. Chimp's shop," he says. "I hope there are still a few left . . ." When the pair arrive, they find Bill Badger and his mother are already there. "Hello, Rupert!" cries Bill. "I've come to buy a pumpkin to make a lantern for Ottoline's party . . ." "So have I!" laughs Rupert. "I hope that isn't the last one."

Rupert arrives to find Bill's Mum
Buying a pumpkin for his chum . . .

RUPERT MAKES A LANTERN

*"I know!" says Mrs. Badger. "I
Can make us all a pumpkin pie!"*

*"Good luck, you two! It's quite a task
To turn a pumpkin to a mask . . ."*

*The pals start working carefully -
"That's right - save the inside for me . . ."*

*They start with eyes - then cut out rows
Of jagged teeth and make a nose . . .*

Luckily for Rupert, Mr. Chimp produces a second pumpkin, so the pals can have one each. "If Rupert comes back to our house you can both make lanterns together!" says Mrs. Badger. "And I can make a pumpkin pie at the same time . . ." "Good idea!" laughs Mr. Bear. "Then nothing will be wasted. Perhaps they could take your pie to the party too." The delighted chums set off across the common towards Bill's house. "See you later!" calls Mr. Bear. "Have fun making the lanterns."

At Bill's house the two chums settle down to start work on their lanterns . . . "Cut off the tops first, then scoop out both pumpkins," says Mrs. Badger. "When you've finished that, you can cut faces in the hollow shells." The pals carefully empty the pumpkins into a bowl, then start work on a pair of frightening faces. "Very good!" smiles Mrs. Badger. "Now I'll find you both candles to go inside. You'll need some string too, for making handles, then you can carry the lanterns along."

*"Thanks, Bill!" calls Rupert. "We can light
Our way with these, tomorrow night!"*

*"Well done!" says Mrs. Bear. "Now you
Will need to choose a costume too . . ."*

*"I'll help you too!" says Mr. Bear.
"You'll need a pointed hat to wear . . ."*

*"A wizard costume!" Rupert tells
His mother he's made up some spells . . .*

Rupert and Bill are thrilled with their lanterns. "They'll look even better when it's dark!" says Rupert. "I can't wait to show mine to everyone else." Mr. Bear is pleased too. "Well done!" he says. "Just the thing for tomorrow night." Remembering Ottoline's party, Rupert asks his mother if she will help him make a costume. "Of course!" she laughs. "What would you like to go as?" Rupert can't decide. "An Egyptian mummy? A skeleton?" Finally, he has a good idea . . .

The next day, Rupert's parents both help him make a costume . . . "Going as a wizard is a splendid idea!" says Mr. Bear. "I agree!" says Rupert's mother. "With a pointed hat and star-spangled gown you'll really look the part!" When everything is ready, Rupert puts on his costume and chants a spell, just like the Chinese Conjurer. "My wand shall summon everyone, to Ottoline's - to join the fun!" "Very good!" laughs Mr. Bear. "Goodness! There's someone at the door already . . ."

RUPERT'S PAL ARRIVES

"Good gracious!" Rupert's father cries
*When Bill arrives in **his** disguise . . .*

"Count Dracula" has brought a pie
For all the party guests to try . . .

The chums set off - their lanterns glow
And light the pathway as they go . . .

Then, suddenly, the pals both see
A stranger. "Look! Who can it be?"

As Mr. Bear opens the door he gives a cry of surprise and starts back in alarm. "Hello, Mr. Bear!" laughs Bill. "Sorry if I scared you! I'm going to the party as Count Dracula . . ." As well as his lantern, Bill is also carrying Mrs. Badger's pumpkin pie, which everyone gathers round to admire. "What a nice idea to take it with you," says Rupert's mother. "I'll say!" nods Mr. Bear. "It looks delicious!" "Time we were going!" says Bill. "I hope my outfit isn't *too* creepy!"

"Goodbye!" calls Mrs. Bear as the pals set off with their pumpkin lanterns glowing. "It's just as well you've got something with you to light the way . . ." Darkness falls as the pair reach the edge of the common and all they can see are the shadows of bushes and trees. "I say!" whispers Bill. "There's someone coming towards us." "You're right!" gasps Rupert. "I wonder who it can be?" "Good evening!" booms a deep voice. "Is this the way to Nutwood's haunted Manor?"

RUPERT AND HIS PALS ARE ROBBED

The "monster" chuckles as he comes
Towards the pair of startled chums . . .

"It's Algy Pug!" laughs Bill. "Trust you
To make a scary costume too . . ."

Two "highwaymen" confront the three -
The Fox twins - hiding by a tree . . .

"Hands up!" calls Freddy. "Trick or treat!"
"We're after booty we can eat . . ."

As the lumbering figure approaches, Bill and Rupert are both convinced he looks oddly familiar . . . "Algy Pug!" laughs Rupert. "Hello!" chuckles his pal. "How do you like my costume? I made the helmet out of cardboard, then dressed up in one of my father's old coats." "Excellent!" says Bill. "You really had me fooled! I'd forgotten how we used to think Nutwood Manor was haunted. That was before Ottoline arrived, of course. There won't be any *real* ghosts there tonight!"

The three pals walk towards Ottoline's house, with the pumpkin lanterns lighting their way. Suddenly, they hear a cry of "Stand and deliver!" as two masked figures jump out from behind a tree. "Freddy and Ferdy!" says Rupert. "They're dressed as highwaymen!" hisses Bill. "Trick or Treat!" says Freddy, pointing a water pistol at the chums. "Hand over your goodies or you're in for a soaking!" "It's only a pie!" protests Bill. "I was going to share it with everybody at the party!"

RUPERT'S CHUMS ARE SOAKED

The Foxes take the pie then say
They'll squirt the three pals anyway . . .

"They don't know when to stop - those two!"
Says Algy. "Now I'm soaked right through!"

The soaking chums complain that their
Costumes are wrecked beyond repair . . .

"Oh, no!" says Ottoline. "Poor you!
Caught by the Foxes' ambush too . . ."

"A pie!" laughs Freddy. "We'll share *that*, won't we Ferdy?" "I'll say!" nods his brother. "Half for you and half for me!" "Give it back!" says Algy, but the Foxes only squirt their water pistols and run away. "We've got a treat and we've played a trick!" chuckles Freddy as the pair disappear. "Trust them!" splutters Algy. "I'm drenched right through!" "Me too!" says Bill. "And they've stolen the pie!" "What a pair!" says Rupert. "They're always up to some sort of silly prank!"

"The Foxes have wrecked my costume!" complains Rupert as the bedraggled chums continue on their way to Nutwood Manor. "Mine too!" says Algy. "The paint has started to run." "Never mind," says Bill. "At least we'll be able to get dry at Ottoline's house. It isn't very far now. I can see it through the trees." "Oh, no!" cries Ottoline when she answers the door. "Freddy and Ferdy have got you too! Those rascals have been squirting guests all evening. I hope you don't catch colds!"

RUPERT HEARS ABOUT THE FOXES

*"The Fox brothers have had their fun
By squirting simply everyone . . ."*

*"But that's not all!" says Rex. "This time
The pair have turned to highway crime!"*

*"They robbed me too!" says Willie. "Then
Just laughed - and squirted me again!"*

*The doorbell rings. It's Gregory -
"Whatever can the matter be?"*

Ottoline tells the chums to take off their wet costumes and dry themselves straightaway. "Rex and Reggie got a soaking from the Foxes too!" she says. "It's such a shame your costumes have all been spoilt . . ." "Hello!" says Rex. "I see that Nutwood's highwaymen have ambushed you too!" "They've gone too far this time!" complains his brother. "Playing jokes is one thing, but they stole the food we were bringing to the party!" "I know!" nods Rupert. "They took Bill's pie as well . . ."

As the chums get dry, the other party guests come to see what has happened . . . "The Foxes robbed me too!" complains Willie Mouse. *"And they gave me a squirting. 'Trick or treat', they said-but I think it's mean!"* Just then, the doorbell rings and Gregory Guineapig appears. "I've been robbed!" he wails. "Two strangers sprang out from the bushes and squirted me with water pistols!" "There, there!" says Ottoline gently. "Come in and get dry. It was only Freddy and Ferdy."

"Two highwaymen! They blocked the way
Then took my party food away . . ."

"Don't worry!" Rupert says. "We'll get
Our own back on the Foxes yet!"

"We'll need balloons! One each will do -
Then I'll explain my plan to you . . ."

Next, Rupert borrows a disguise -
"To take the Foxes by surprise!"

"They took my tin of biscuits!" sobs Gregory. "I made them specially for the party - now nobody will even see what they were like!" "Don't worry!" says Rupert. "We're going to get *everything* back and teach the Foxes a lesson!" "How?" asks Bill. "We'll play a trick on them!" declares Rupert. "All this dressing up in costumes has given me a good idea. We'll have to be quick, though. Everything depends on taking Freddy and Ferdy by surprise. Gather round and I'll tell you what I need . . ."

When everyone is ready, Rupert begins to explain his plan to trick the Foxes . . . "The first thing I want is balloons!" he tells Ottoline. "That's easy!" she says. "There's a spare packet we haven't opened yet . . ." "Good!" says Rupert. "You'll all need one each." The next thing he asks for is Bingo's ghost costume. "It should be just the right size." he smiles. "Right for what?" blinks the brainy pup. "Me!" laughs Rupert. "I'll need a good disguise to play the Foxes at their own game."

Rupert and the Pumpkin Pie

RUPERT SETS OUT IN DISGUISE

The chums all file out silently -
"This way!" says Rupert. "Follow me . . ."

"Find hiding places, everyone.
*This time it's **our** turn to have fun!"*

Then Rupert waits until he sees
The Foxes, moving through the trees . . .

He puts on Bingo's costume, then
Walks back to Ottoline's again . . .

Shortly after Rupert has explained his plan, a strange procession moves silently away from Nutwood Manor . . . "We'll cut across the common!" hisses Rupert. "Quiet as you can now, everyone." The pals follow Rupert until they reach the start of the path to Ottoline's house. "This looks a good spot!" he says. "I'll get ready, while you all find places to hide. Whatever happens, don't come out until you hear me call!" "Right!" nods Bill as he and Podgy duck behind a tree . . .

No sooner has the last of his chums taken shelter, than Rupert spots two familiar-looking figures, lurking by the side of the road. "Freddy and Ferdy!" he gasps. "I *knew* they'd still be on the prowl! I'd better get ready for them straightaway." Draped in Bingo's ghostly costume, Rupert is impossible to recognise. Carrying a basket of goodies, he sets off along the path towards Nutwood Manor, as if he was arriving at the fancy-dress party for the first time . . .

The Foxes jump out. "Stop!" they cry
As Ottoline's new guest goes by . . .

"Shan't!" Rupert says and runs away.
The Foxes call for him to stay.

"Just wait!" calls Freddy. "Nobody
Escapes from us that easily!"

Then Rupert stops. He turns around,
Throws off the sheet and stands his ground!

As Rupert passes by, the Fox brothers jump out, waving their water pistols. "Stop!" calls Ferdy. "Trick or Treat!" cries his brother. "Hand over your basket, whoever you are . . ." "Shan't!" replies Rupert. "Ghosts aren't frightened by footpad foxes! You'll have to catch me, if you can . . ." Freddy and Ferdy are so surprised that they don't even squirt Rupert as he hurries away. "Hey! Wait!" calls Freddy. "We know you're not *really* a ghost. Come back and give us those goodies."

Rupert runs off along the path, with the Fox brothers close behind . . . "You won't get away that easily!" warns Freddy. "Halloween's the night for tricks and nobody out-tricks us . . ." Suddenly, Rupert stops and throws off his ghostly disguise. "That's where you're wrong!" he laughs. "Rupert!" blinks Ferdy. "But you've already been to Ottoline's party!" "That's right!" nods his brother. "We caught him with Bill and Algy Pug. What's going on? Why are you wearing another costume?"

RUPERT TRICKS THE FOX BROTHERS

He laughs as the dumbfounded pair
See all the Nutwood chums are there . . .

"A trap!" cries Freddy Fox. "Oh, no!
They've all brought water bombs to throw!"

"Take that!" calls Reggie. "Serves you right!
The Fox Brothers are put to flight . . .

"A pond!" wails Freddy. "Ferdy, wait!"
The pair can't stop though, it's too late!

To the Foxes' astonishment, they suddenly find themselves surrounded by guests from Ottoline's party. "This time, we've tricked you!" laughs Rupert. Each pal is carrying a large balloon filled with water . . . "Help!" cries Ferdy, but it is too late. Water bombs sail towards the pair from every side, drenching them to the skin. "Take that!" cries Bill. "And this!" calls Ottoline. "There are plenty more treats for you two. Everyone *you* squirted has come to get their revenge!"

"Stop!" cries Ferdy. "It's not fair!" "Oh, yes it is!" laughs Reggie Rabbit. "You just don't like it when other people are playing tricks on *you* . . ." "Run for it!" calls Freddy, dashing off through the trees. Ferdy follows close behind, but in the darkness the pair lose their way and plunge straight into a muddy pond. "I can't stop!" gasps Freddy. "Neither can I!" wails Ferdy. One after the other, they slip on the mud and go tumbling forward, into the icy water . . .

RUPERT ENJOYS THE PARTY

"It's your turn now!" laughs Gregory.
"Just like when you both squirted me!"

"Come on!" says Rupert. "Everyone
Is even now. We've had our fun ..."

The Foxes promise to restore
The stolen party gifts once more ...

They dry themselves, then both join in
Just as the party treats begin ...

"No more!" pleads Freddy as the chums all gather round. "Now you know what it's like!" says Bill. "Exactly!" nods Gregory. "It's not so much fun when you're on the receiving end, is it?" "No!" shivers Ferdy. "And we're even colder and wetter than you were!" "Come on!" laughs Rupert, hauling him up to his feet. "We've *all* had enough of pranks for one night, I think. You'd better get changed and dry before you both catch dreadful colds. Come with us, back to Ottoline's party ..."

On the way back to Nutwood Manor, Freddy and Ferdy stop to retrieve the stolen goodies. "Bravo!" smiles Rupert. "Now we'll *all* be able to have a slice of pumpkin pie ..." Mrs. Otter wraps the pair in dressing gowns and puts their clothes to dry by the fire. "I hope you've had fun!" she asks. "Yes, thanks!" laughs Rupert. "We've finished with tricks till next Halloween and there are plenty of treats here for everyone!"

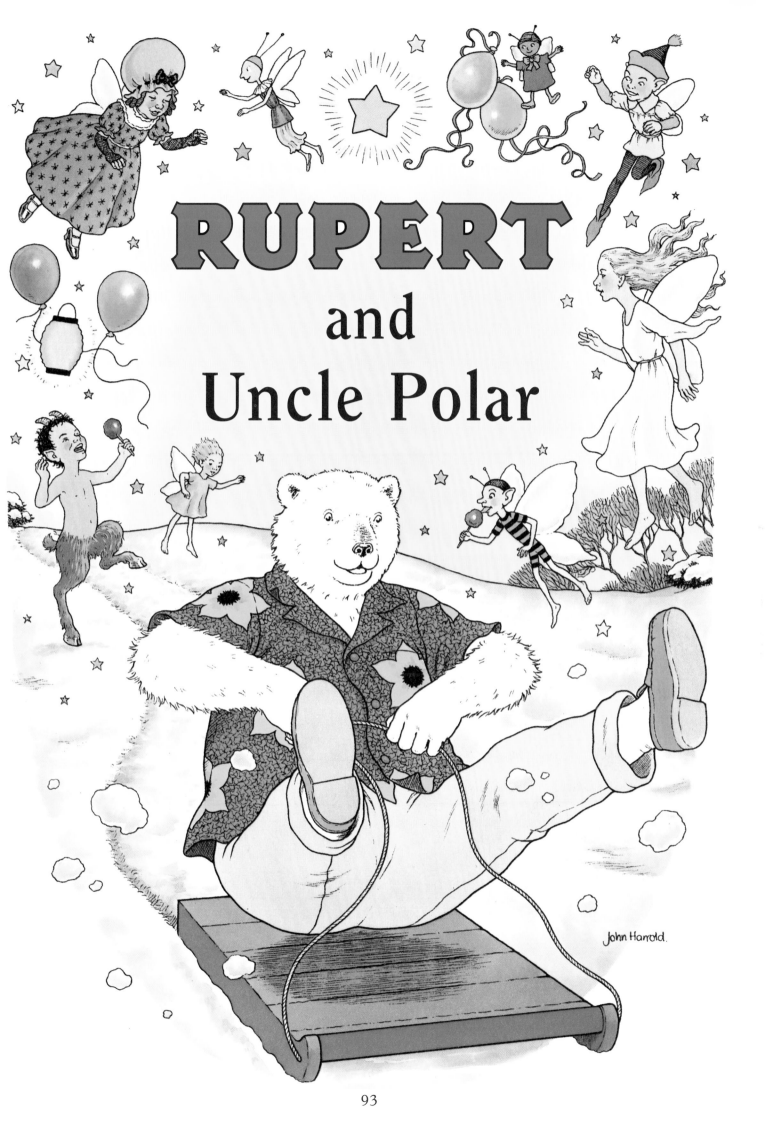

RUPERT
and
Uncle Polar

John Harrold.

RUPERT PREPARES FOR A VISITOR

"Your Uncle Polar's on his way
To Nutwood for a holiday . . ."

"He likes the weather cold, you know,
It's lucky that we're due some snow!"

Next morning, Mr. Bear's proved right -
The whole of Nutwood's snowy white . . .

The Bears are all surprised by how
Much colder Nutwood's feeling now!

It is the middle of Christmas and Rupert and his mother are busy preparing the guest room . . . "I wonder what Polar will think of Nutwood?" smiles Mrs. Bear. "We've invited him before but he only really likes it when there's lots of snow and ice." "There's plenty of that at the North Pole," says Rupert. "Even his house is made out of ice!" As Rupert goes to bed that night, Mr. Bear checks the barometer. "Snow!" he announces. "Just in time for Polar's visit . . ."

Next morning, when Rupert looks out of the window, he sees that the barometer was right. The whole of Nutwood is covered in a thick blanket of crisp, white snow! After breakfast, the Bears get ready to go and meet their visitor at the railway station. "Make sure you wrap up well!" warns Rupert's mother. "There's a chilly wind blowing and it might even snow again!" "It is cold!" says Mr. Bear as the three set out. "Perfect weather for Uncle Polar! He'll really feel at home."

RUPERT'S UNCLE ARRIVES

At Nutwood station, Rupert hears
A whistle blow - the train appears . . .

"Hello there!" Polar gives a call.
"It's nice to finally see you all!"

"My little nephew! Let me see -
You'll soon have grown as tall as me!"

"Phew!" Polar gasps. "It's so hot here!
Where I come from, it snows all year . . ."

When Rupert and his parents arrive at the station, they find that Uncle Polar's train has been delayed by snow. At last the station-master announces that it will be the next one to arrive. "I can see it coming now!" calls Rupert excitedly. "Look!" The train stops and a familiar figure steps out on to the platform. "Uncle Polar!" calls Rupert. "Over here! We've come to meet you . . ." "Wonderful!" beams Polar. "I've been travelling for so long I can hardly believe I've arrived!"

"Nutwood at last!" laughs Polar as he lifts Rupert into the air. "What a journey I've had to get here! First I travelled by sleigh, then on a ship and finally by train . . ." "You've certainly brought some arctic weather with you!" says Mr. Bear. "This must be one of the heaviest snowfalls we've had for years." As he walks back from the station, Uncle Polar takes out a handkerchief and mops his brow. "Phew!" he puffs. "It might be cold for you, but in the arctic we'd call this a heatwave!"

RUPERT FEELS HOT

At Rupert's, Uncle Polar goes
Upstairs to change his travelling clothes . . .

"That's better! Now I feel just right -
This summer outfit's nice and light!"

Outside, he basks in Nutwood's sun
While Rupert joins him. "This is fun!"

"Can we go sledging in the snow?"
"Yes!" Polar smiles. "I'd love to go . . ."

As soon as the Bears get home, Rupert's father hurries off to stoke the fire. Mrs. Bear shows Polar to his room, then says she'll make a cup of tea. "That would be nice!" says Rupert's uncle. "If you don't mind, I think I'll change out of my travelling clothes and join you in a moment." To Rupert's surprise, his uncle reappears, wearing a brightly patterned, short-sleeved shirt . . . "That's much better!" he smiles. "The weather's so mild here in Nutwood it feels like the middle of summer!"

After tea, Rupert decides to build a snowman in the garden. "I'll come and help!" says Polar. As Rupert adds the finishing touches, his uncle declares the weather's so mild he's going to bask in the sun. "Delightful!" he sighs. "I don't know why I've never done this before . . ." A little later, Rupert shows Uncle Polar the new sledge he had for Christmas. "Can we go for a ride on the common?" he asks. "Of course!" laughs Polar. "I'd love to! We can set off straightaway . . ."

RUPERT GOES TOBOGGANING

*"When I was a young cub like you
I used to ride toboggans too!"*

*"A trail of footprints! Let me see -
I'll try to guess whose they could be . . ."*

*"Two friends out sledging left this trail -
The smaller of them has a tail . . ."*

*"It's Willie Mouse!" gasps Rupert. "There,
With Podgy . . . **They** must be the pair!"*

"I wonder if we'll see anyone else on the common?" says Rupert. "All my chums enjoy tobogganing too! Whenever it snows we like to have races." "That sounds fun!" smiles Polar. "I used to have a toboggan when I was a cub, you know! Up in the arctic you can use them all year round . . ." As the pair climb to the top of the hill, Uncle Polar points to a trail of footprints in the snow. "Somebody else has been tobogganing too!" he laughs. "Let's take a closer look . . ."

"You can tell a lot from marks in the snow!" says Uncle Polar. "In the arctic it's one of the main ways of finding your way about." Kneeling down to examine the footprints, he asks Rupert how many people he thinks have been past. "Two!" says Rupert. "Well done!" cries Polar. "One of them is small and light, with a long tail, while the other is much heavier. They've both been pulling sledges . . ." "Podgy Pig and Willie Mouse!" laughs Rupert as the pair come into view.

*"You have to read the clues to find
Who's left a trail of prints behind . . ."*

*The chums meet Uncle Polar, then
Go back to sledging once again.*

*"Yippee!" calls Rupert, joining in.
"Well done!" cheers Polar, with a grin.*

*"It's **your** turn Uncle! I can tell
You'd like to have a ride as well . . ."*

"I guessed one was a mouse!" laughs Uncle Polar. "I could see where his tail had been trailing along in the snow . . ." "I didn't notice that," says Rupert. "Not many people would!" says Polar. "Looking at footprints takes a bit of practice." Rupert introduces his uncle to the two chums. "Do you *really* live at the North Pole?" asks Willie. "Yes," says Polar. "It's always snowy there." "*We* only get snow once a year!" says Podgy. "That's why it's so exciting . . ."

Polar watches delightedly as the three chums set off on their toboggans down a nearby hill. "Yippee!" cries Rupert. "Race you to the bottom!" When they reach the foot of the hill, Rupert and his chums turn round and haul their sledges back to the top. "Would *you* like a ride this time?" Rupert asks his uncle. "If you're sure I won't be too heavy," says Polar. "I must say it looks fun!" "Climb on and we'll give you a push!" says Willie. "Thanks!" laughs Polar. "I'll start from here . . ."

RUPERT'S UNCLE HAS A GO

"All right!" laughs Polar. "Here I go!
Stand clear, you three! Watch out below . . ."

"Oh, no!" they gasp, dismayed to see
The sledge ride end disastrously!

"Don't look so worried, everyone!"
Laughs Uncle Polar. "No harm done!"

"I say! Let's play a snow game now!
Like Hide and Seek - I'll show you how . . ."

Rupert's uncle sits on the sledge and is given a flying send-off by the three chums . . . "Look out below!" he calls as he speeds downhill. The extra weight makes Polar's ride one the fastest that Rupert has ever seen. "Keep going!" he cheers. "You're doing brilliantly!" Suddenly, Uncle Polar gives a cry of dismay. The sledge tips forward, then flies up into the air, sending him sprawling. "Oh, no!" gasps Rupert, hurrying forward in alarm, "I hope Uncle Polar's all right!"

To Rupert's relief, Polar sits up and shakes the snow from his fur. "Lucky it was a soft landing!" he laughs. "I must be out of practice to tumble off like that, but it was great fun, all the same . . ." As the chums gather round, Rupert's uncle suggests a game of hide and seek. "It's more interesting in snow," he explains. "You have to follow tracks and footprints until you find the person you're after. I played it a lot when I was young. It's not as easy as it sounds."

RUPERT PLAYS HIDE AND SEEK

The game starts - Rupert tip-toes back.
"This way they'll never spot my track!"

He hides behind a bush. "Teehee!
I'm sure they won't discover me . . ."

"It's worked!" thinks Rupert as he waits.
His Uncle stops and hesitates . . .

Then Uncle Polar turns and strides
Straight to the spot where Rupert hides!

All the chums agree that hide and seek in the snow sounds fun. "Rupert can hide first!" declares Polar. "We'll count to one hundred, then see if we can follow his tracks . . ." As his uncle speaks, Rupert suddenly has a good idea. "I know!" he smiles. "Ordinary footprints are easy to follow, but what if I try walking backwards?" Glancing over his shoulder to see the way, Rupert sets off towards a nearby clump of bushes. "They'll never think of looking for me here!" he chuckles.

"Coming!" calls Willie as the chums stop counting. Peeping out from his hiding-place, Rupert can see everyone searching for footprints. Podgy and Willie are easily fooled by Rupert's trick and go wandering off in completely the wrong direction. Uncle Polar seems baffled too. For a long time he looks at the criss-cross tracks in the snow, then peers thoughtfully into the distance. To Rupert's surprise, he suddenly turns and walks straight to his nephew's hide-out . . .

RUPERT'S UNCLE HIDES

*"Well done!" he laughs. "I nearly went
The wrong way too and lost the scent . . ."*

*It's Polar's turn next. "Search the snow
For clues to find which way I go . . ."*

*"Time's up!" calls Rupert. "Let's look round
And find out where he's gone to ground."*

*"Look at these footprints!" Podgy cries.
"I think they're just your uncle's size!"*

"Well done, Rupert!" laughs Uncle Polar. "Your trick nearly fooled us all. It's just the sort of thing my Eskimo friends do, up in the frozen North." Podgy and Willie are keen to try again and urge Uncle Polar to take a turn at hiding. "Very well!" he laughs. "But you might be searching for quite a while. It won't be easy to find me, you know!" Rupert, Willie and Podgy close their eyes and start to count. "See you later!" calls Polar. "Don't forget to search the snow for clues."

By the time that Rupert has finished counting, Uncle Polar is nowhere to be seen. "I wonder where he's hiding?" says Willie. "Let's look at the snow," suggests Rupert. "He said we might spot some clues . . ." At first the search seems hopeless. Rupert follows a trail of footprints, only to find that they're his own! Then Willie points to some more footprints. "They're too big to be mine!" says Podgy. "Or mine!" says the little Mouse. "Rupert! I think we've found your uncle's trail!"

RUPERT FOLLOWS HIS TRAIL

At first the trail is crisp and clear
But then it seems to disappear!

A little bird begins to speak -
"I see you're playing hide and seek . . ."

"I saw which way your uncle took -
Come on! I'll show you where to look!"

"He rubbed his footprints out - and then
Set off along this way again . . ."

At first, Rupert and his chums can follow Uncle Polar's footprints easily but to their surprise they suddenly find that the trail has disappeared . . . "We'll have to look more carefully!" says Rupert. "I'll go this way, while you two try the other direction." As he approaches a clump of bushes all Rupert can see are the marks left by a little bird. "No sign of Polar here!" he murmurs, "I wonder where he's gone?" "Playing hide and seek?" chirps the bird. "Perhaps I can help you . . ."

The bird asks Rupert to describe who he is looking for. "That's him!" it trills. "I noticed the bright plumage! Follow me and I'll show you where he went . . ." Rupert runs after the little bird but is mystified that there is still no sign of Polar's footprints. "He didn't leave any!" laughs the bird. "Rubbed them out behind him, you see?" Rupert spots an old branch lying on the snow. "Of course!" he smiles. "Polar must have used this like a broom . . ."

RUPERT FINDS A HIDDEN CAVE

*"What fun!" thinks Rupert. "I can see
The way to go now easily . . ."*

*Then suddenly he stops and blinks -
"Skidmarks! He's had a fall!" he thinks.*

*The marks show Rupert where to go -
And something hidden in the snow . . .*

*"A cave! He's fallen in! Oh, dear!
It's Rupert, Uncle! Can you hear?"*

Now Rupert can see Polar's footprints again, he feels sure that his uncle will be easy to find. "All I have to do is follow the trail," he smiles. "I can't wait to see his face when I finally track him down." Uncle Polar's footprints lead Rupert to a high, wooded hill. "How different everything looks in the snow!" he marvels. Setting off downhill, Rupert stops suddenly and stares at the tracks in dismay. "Polar must have lost his footing!" he gasps. "He's tumbled over and slid all the way down!"

Following the marks in the snow, Rupert clambers carefully down the hill in search of his uncle. When he reaches the bottom, he is amazed to find that the trail ends by a jagged hole in the snow, which reveals the mouth of a hidden cave . . . "He's fallen in!" gasps Rupert. "I hope he isn't hurt! I'd better call down and let him know I'm here." Kneeling by the cave mouth, he calls out Polar's name, but receives no reply. "Uncle Polar!" he calls again. "Can you hear me? It's Rupert . . ."

RUPERT HAS A FALL

*As Rupert tries another call
Some snow breaks off - he starts to fall . . .*

*He tumbles over, round and round,
And ends up in the cave he's found!*

*"Oh, no!" groans Rupert. "**I'm** trapped now!
"I've got to get back out, but how?"*

*"A tunnel!" Rupert wonders where
It leads to . . . "Perhaps Polar's there?"*

Rupert listens anxiously by the hole in the snow, but all he can hear is his own voice, echoing in the cavern below. Leaning forward, he peers into the gloom but can see no sign of Uncle Polar. Suddenly a mass of overhanging snow breaks away and catches Rupert off balance. With a startled cry he topples headlong into the cave in a flurry of snow and ice. "I can't stop!" gasps Rupert as he plunges down the narrow shaft, going faster and faster, tumbling helplessly head over heels . . .

To Rupert's relief, his fall is cushioned by a deep pile of snow. "At least that's something!" he blinks, but as he looks up he sees that the opening in the snow has been reduced to a tiny gap that is too small for him to climb back out. Clambering to his feet, he looks around to find that the cave is really a long underground tunnel, leading far off into the distance . . . "I wonder if that's where Uncle Polar's gone?" he thinks. "I'll just peek round the corner to see if there's any sign."

RUPERT MAKES A DISCOVERY

*"Music!" blinks Rupert. "I can hear
A fiddle playing, somewhere near . . ."*

*Then Rupert stares in shocked surprise -
He shakes his head and rubs his eyes . . .*

*"A frozen lake, where Autumn Elves
Go skating and enjoy themselves!"*

*"Hello!" their Chief laughs. "Come and play!
Our Ice Fair only lasts one day!"*

As Rupert walks towards the end of the tunnel he suddenly hears music playing and the sound of voices . . . "A fiddler!" he gasps. "He's playing a jig!" Lantern light glows from the cavern which Rupert approaches and the noise of voices and laughter increases with every step. "I wonder who it can be?" he blinks. "It sounds a bit like a party, but I can't think who would be holding one down here, underground." Stepping into the cavern, he stares delightedly in astonished surprise . . .

Blinking in disbelief, Rupert finds himself by the edge of a frozen lake, watching skaters and merrymakers of all kinds . . . "Autumn Elves!" he murmurs, "But what are they all doing?" "Rupert!" cries the Chief Elf. "Fancy meeting *you* here! I didn't realise you knew about the Ice Fair." "I don't! At least, I *didn't*," marvels Rupert. "The music sounded lively, but I'd no idea I'd discover anything like this!" "Happens every winter!" smiles the Elf. "To celebrate the New Year . . ."

RUPERT SPOTS UNCLE POLAR

"We hold an Ice Fair every year
To celebrate when Spring is near . . ."

As Rupert takes a look around
He spots his uncle - safe and sound!

"Hey! Uncle Polar! I'm here too!
I scrambled down to look for you . . ."

"I'm sorry, Nephew! It was wrong
Of me to linger here so long . . ."

As the Chief Elf shows him round the Ice Fair, Rupert spots visitors from all over Nutwood and far beyond . . . "Woodland creatures of every kind come to the Fair," explains his guide. "We all like a day of fun to make up for the Winter gloom!" On the way to the toffee-apple stall Rupert spots a familiar figure, taking part in the curling. "Uncle Polar!" he laughs. "So that's where he got to after he fell through the snow! I might have known he'd be all right!"

Rupert hurries across the ice to greet his uncle. "I've found you at last!" he cries. "Hello!" smiles Polar. "I'm sorry I didn't come back straightaway, but I tumbled through the snow and found the Fair in full swing! Couldn't resist trying my luck at the curling. Up at the North Pole it's one of our favourite games . . ." "Do you think there's time for a look round before we go?" asks Rupert hopefully. "I don't see why not!" smiles his uncle. "After all, the Fair only happens once a year!"

RUPERT WINS A PRIZE

Before they leave for home, the pair
Take one last look around the Fair . . .

They come across a skittle stall -
"A prize if you can make three fall!"

The lady says that Rupert's won
Himself a silver star. "Well done!"

"It's time for us to get back now..."
The Chief Elf says he'll show them how.

Rupert and his uncle are astonished by the sights and sounds of the Ice Fair. Musicians play and skaters glide, while stall after stall offers games to play and treats to eat. "How about skittles?" suggests a lady. "Four balls each and three strikes to win!" Rupert steps forward excitedly and takes careful aim. "Bravo!" cheers Polar as first one and then a second skittle falls. Rupert tries again but this time throws too high. "Last chance!" says Polar. "See what you can do . . ."

To Rupert's delight, his final throw hits a skittle too and the lady in charge of the stall declares he has won a prize. "A silver star!" she smiles and pins it to his coat. "Well done!" says Polar. "But I'm afraid it's time we went back to look for your friends . . ." "This way," says the Chief Elf, when he hears how the pair's way in has been blocked by a fall of snow. "There are many ways back to Nutwood, but you have to be an Imp or an Elf to find them."

RUPERT RETURNS TO THE COMMON

"This way!" the Elf calls. "Follow me!
These steps lead to a hollow tree."

The pair climb through a secret door,
Back up above the ground once more . . .

The other two are startled when
They see that Rupert's back again . . .

"It's quite a story!" Rupert smiles.
"I followed Polar's trail for miles!"

"I'd no idea there were so many tunnels under the common!" says Uncle Polar as the Chief Elf leads them back. "In every direction!" laughs the Elf. "There's a map of them all at Elfin H.Q. Jolly useful for getting about without being seen . . ." After a while, they reach a steep flight of steps, which leads to a circular door. "Nutwood common!" announces the Chief. "I'm glad you enjoyed the Fair. Come next year, if you like. At the end of the old year and the start of the new!"

As the door in the tree swings shut behind them, Rupert and his uncle spot a familiar pair, still peering at tracks in the snow. "*There* you are!" cries Willie. "But wherever did you get to? Podgy and I looked everywhere we could think of but we couldn't find a single clue!" "It's a long story!" laughs Rupert. "You'll never believe what we found! Let's warm up with a cup of tea while I tell you all about it . . ."

Follow Rupert every day

John Harrold.

in The Express

ANSWERS TO PUZZLES:

(P.75) SPOT THE DIFFERENCE:
1. Ribbon missing from Bill's parcel; 2. Stripe missing from Bill's trousers; 3. Doorknob missing; 4. Streamer missing (above Willie Mouse); 5. Headlamp missing from Rupert's toy car; 6. Picture missing from frame; 7. Cake missing from plate; 8. Bingo's bow-tie missing; 9. Balloon missing (above Bingo); 10. Mrs. Bear's brooch missing.

(P.77) CROSSWORD

Across
1. Ferdy, 2. List, 4. Edward, 5. Nutwood, 9. Dracula, 11. Bodkin, 12. Cold, 13. Bingo, 14. Igloo, 16. Wet, 17. Joan, 18. Ice, 19. Open, 21. Cakeville, 22. Raft, 24. Skittles, 27. Brown, 28. Bear, 29. Odmedod, 30. Melt, 32. Sage of Um, 34. Horse, 35. Algy, 36. Crown, 37. Curling.

Down
1. Freddy, 3. Sun, 6. Unicorn, 7. Ottoline, 8. Halloween, 10. Uncle Polar, 15. Orange, 17. January, 20. Willie Mouse, 23. Toucan, 24. Scarecrow, 25. Snowman, 26. Weather, 31. Lemon, 33. Gold.

(P.79) WHICH STORY?
(1)P.41 (2)P.66 (3)P.50 (4)P.30 (5)P.71 (6)P.27 (7)P.13 (8)P.41 (9)P.7 (10)P.108 (11)P.17 (12)P.58 (13)P.108 (14)P.46 (15)P.25 (16) P.59